MW00617165

La Cage Aux Folles

Music and Lyrics   Book
Jerry Herman   Harvey Fierstein

Based on the Play *La Cage aux Folles* by Jean Poiret

A SAMUEL FRENCH ACTING EDITION

SAMUEL
FRENCH
FOUNDED 1830

SAMUELFRENCH.COM
SAMUELFRENCH-LONDON.CO.UK

FOR PRODUCTION ENQUIRIES

UNITED STATES AND CANADA
Info@SamuelFrench.com
1-866-598-8449

UNITED KINGDOM AND EUROPE
Plays@SamuelFrench-London.co.uk
020-7255-4302

Each title is subject to availability from Samuel French, depending upon
country of performance. Please be aware that LA CAGE AUX FOLLES
may not be licensed by Samuel French in your territory. Professional
and amateur producers should contact the nearest Samuel French
office or licensing partner to verify availability.

MUSIC USE NOTE

Licensees are solely responsible for obtaining formal written permission from copyright owners to use copyrighted music in the performance of this play and are strongly cautioned to do so. If no such permission is obtained by the licensee, then the licensee must use only original music that the licensee owns and controls. Licensees are solely responsible and liable for all music clearances and shall indemnify the copyright owners of the play(s) and their licensing agent, Samuel French, against any costs, expenses, losses and liabilities arising from the use of music by licensees. Please contact the appropriate music licensing authority in your territory for the rights to any incidental music.

MUSIC COPYRIGHT

Musical Numbers:
"We Are What We Are"
"Mascara"
"Song on the Sand"
"La Cage Aux Folles"
"I Am What I Am"
"Masculinity"
"Look Over There"
"Fugue (Canon)" ["Cocktail Counterpoint"]
"Promenade"
"The Best of Times"
"With Anne on My Arm"

RENTAL MATERIALS

An orchestration consisting of **Full Conductor Score, Keyboard 2/ Conductor Score, Keyboard 1, Woodwind 1, Woodwind 2, Trumpet, Trombone, Drums,** and **Double Bass** will be loaned two months prior to the production ONLY on the receipt of the Licensing Fee quoted for all performances, the rental fee and a refundable deposit.

Please contact Samuel French for perusal of the music materials as well as a performance license application.

Allan Carr originally produced *La Cage aux Folles* on Broadway with Kenneth-Mark Productions, Marvin A. Kraus, Stewart F. Lane, James M. Nederlander, Martin Richards, and as executive producers, Barry Brown and Fritz Holt.

This version of the script was developed and performed during the 2009 West End and 2011 Broadway revival

IMPORTANT BILLING AND CREDIT REQUIREMENTS

All producers of *LA CAGE AUX FOLLES must* give credit to the Author(s) of the Play(s) in all programs distributed in connection with performances of the Play(s), and in all instances in which the title of the Play(s) appears for the purposes of advertising, publicizing or otherwise exploiting the Play(s) and/or a production.

The Authors' billing must appear immediately after the title of the Play, with no matter appearing between the title and the billing, on two separate lines (the first line to indicate respective authorship and the second to contain the name of the respective Authors) with the billing for Jerry Herman on the left side of both lines and the billing for Harvey Fierstein on the right side of both lines, and with no other names or matter appearing on such lines or preceding the Authors' names except the name(s) of star(s), if any, appearing above the title of the play and the name of the producer above the title. The placement of the Authors' credits to appear as follows:

LA CAGE AUX FOLLES (100%)

Music and Lyrics by	Book by (37½%)
JERRY HERMAN	HARVEY FIERSTEIN (75%)

The size of the billing given to the Authors must be the same and in no event less than 75% with respect to their names and 37½% with respect to their authorship contribution of the type size used for the largest letter used in the particular advertising of publicity for the title of the Play. No billing may appear in type larger or more prominent than the billing to the Authors except for the title of the Play. In addition, only stars may receive billing as large and prominent as the Authors. No more than two stars may receive billing above the title of the Play. No billing box may be used. No person (including, without limitation, the producer) may be accorded possessory credit (e.g. "Director's Production of" or "Producer's Production of" with the title of the Play. The following credit must be accorded wherever and whenever the names of the Authors appear, on a separate line immediately beneath the Author's credit and at SO% of the size and prominence of the Authors' credit:

Based on the Play "La Cage aux Folles"   by JEAN POIRET

18¾%   37½%

Notwithstanding the foregoing, the producer is not required to give M. Poiret such billing credit on marquees or in ABC ads of less than two column inches.

LA CAGE AUX FOLLES was first produced at the Palace Theatre in New York City on August 21, 1983. The performance was directed by Arthur Laurents, with sets by David Mitchell, costumes by Theoni V. Aldredge, lighting by Jules Fisher, sound by Peter J. Fitzgerald, hair and makeup by Ted Azar, and choregoraphy by Scott Salmon. The cast was as follows:

GEORGES	Gene Barry
CHANTAL	David Cahn
MONIQUE	Dennis Callahan
DERMAH	Ftank DiPasquale
NICOLE	John Dolf
HANNA	David Engel
MERCEDES	David Evans
BITELLE	Linda Haberman
LO SINGH	Eric Lamp
ODETTE	Dan O'Grady
ANGELIQUE	Deborah Phelan
PHAEDRA	David Scala
CLO-CLO	Sam Singhaus
FRANCIS	Brian Kelly
JACOB	William Thomas, Jr.
ALBIN	George Hearn
JEAN-MICHEL	John Weiner
ANNE	Leslie Stevens
JACQUELINE	Elizabeth Parrish
M. RENAUD	Walter Charles
MME. RENAUD	Sydney Anderson
PAULETTE	Betsy Craig
HERCULE	Jack Neubeck
ETIENNE	Jay Pierce
BABETTE	Marie Santell
COLETTE	Jennifer Smith
TABARRO	Mark Waldrop
PEPE	Ken Ward
EDOUARD DINDON	Jay Garner
MME. DINDON	Merle Louise
SWING PERFORMERS	Bob Brubach, Drew Geraci, Jan Leigh Herndon, Leslie Simons

SONIA FRIEDMAN PRODUCTIONS, DAVID BABANI, BARRY and FRAN WEISSLER and
EDWIN W. SCHLOSS, BOB BARTNER/NORMAN TULCHIN, BROADWAY ACROSS AMERICA, MATTHEW MITCHELL,
RAISE THE ROOF 4 RICHARD WINKLER/BENSINGER TAYLOR/LAUDENSLAGER BERGÈRE,
ARLENE SCANLAN/JOHN O'BOYLE, INDEPENDENT PRESENTERS NETWORK, OLYMPUS THEATRICALS,
ALLEN SPIVAK, JERRY FRANKEL/BAT-BARRY PRODUCTIONS, NEDERLANDER PRESENTATIONS, INC/HARVEY WEINSTEIN

Present the MENIER CHOCOLATE FACTORY Production

KELSEY GRAMMER

with

DOUGLAS HODGE

in

LA CAGE AUX FOLLES

MUSIC & LYRICS BY
JERRY HERMAN

BOOK BY
HARVEY FIERSTEIN

BASED ON THE PLAY "LA CAGE AUX FOLLES" BY **JEAN POIRET**

Starring
FRED   VEANNE
APPLEGATE   COX

CHRIS   ELENA   A.J.
HOCH   SHADDOW   SHIVELY

with

CHRISTINE ANDREAS

and

ROBIN De JESÚS

DALE HENSLEY	HEATHER LINDELL	CAITLIN MUNDTH	BILL NOLTE	DAVID NATHAN PERLOW	CHERYL STERN

And featuring the notorious and dangerous Cagelles

NICK ADAMS	CHRISTOPHE CABALLERO	SEAN A. CARMON	NICHOLAS CUNNINGHAM	SEAN PATRICK DOYLE	LOGAN KESLAR	TODD LATTIMORE	TERRY LAVELL

Scenic Design	Costume Design	Lighting Design	Sound Design	Wig & Makeup Design
TIM SHORTALL	MATTHEW WRIGHT	NICK RICHINGS	JONATHAN DEANS	RICHARD MAWBEY

Associate Choreographer	Technical Supervisors	Production Stage Manager	Associate Producers
NICHOLAS CUNNINGHAM	ARTHUR SICCARDI & PATRICK SULLIVAN	KRISTEN HARRIS	CARLOS ARANA ROBERT DRIEMEYER

Music Director
TODD ELLISON

Musical Coordinator
JOHN MILLER

Casting	Press Representative	Advertising	UK General Management
DUNCAN STEWART	BONEAU/BRYAN-BROWN	SPOTCO	DIANE BENJAMIN, PAM SKINNER & TOM SIRACUSA

General Manager
B.J. HOLT

Executive Producer
ALECIA PARKER

Music Supervision, Orchestrations & Dance Arrangements
JASON CARR

Choreography by
LYNNE PAGE

Directed by
TERRY JOHNSON

This production premiered at the Menier Chocolate Factory November 23, 2007
and transferred to the Playhouse Theatre October 30, 2008.
Original Chocolate Factory Set Design by David Farley.

PRINCIPAL CHARACTERS

ALBIN – a performer of star quality; mature; great powerhouse of a Broadway voice; fine comic actor.

GEORGES – a star, mature and attractive; good singer; energetic, loving and caring; must move well.

JEAN-MICHEL – must appear to be 20 years old; handsome, brunette, masculine, well-mannered, educated; desperately in love with his fiancee, Anne; lyric baritone who acts, sings, and moves well.

JACOB – Black male butler/maid in his early 20's; brilliant comedian who sings and moves well.

ANNE – 18-21; Jean-Michel's fiancee; lovely to look at; spunky; a superb dancer who acts well.

DINDON – Anne's father; right-wing radical politician; pompous; quirky; must sing, move well, and be a fine comedian.

MARIE DINDON – Anne's mother; 48-52, shy, retiring, sexually repressed and sex-starved; good singer and actress who moves well; must look great in a leotard for the finale.

JACQUELINE – mature, female friend of Georges and Albin; owns a chic restaurant; attractive, charming; very theatrical; not necessarily a singer.

RENAUD – mature, male friend of Georges and Albin; owns a small cafe; understudies both of the leads.

FRANCIS – male stage manager in Georges' club; strong actor/dancer.

SETTING
St. Tropez, France

TIME
Summer

MUSICAL NUMBERS

ACT ONE

"Prologue". . . . . ORCHESTRA

"We Are What We Are" . . . . LES CAGELLES

"A Little More Mascara" . . . . .ALBIN & FRIENDS

"With Anne on My Arm" . . . . JEAN-MICHEL

"With You on My Arm". . . . . .GEORGES & ALBIN

"The Promenade" . . . . .TOWNSPEOPLE

"Song on the Sand". . . . . GEORGES

"La Cage aux Folles". . . . . ALBIN, LES CAGELLES

"I Am What I Am". . . . . ALBIN

ACT TWO

"Entr'acte" . . . . ORCHESTRA

"Song on the Sand" reprise . . . . .GEORGES & ALBIN

"Masculinity" . . . . GEORGES, ALBIN & TOWNSPEOPLE

"Look Over There" . . . . .GEORGES

"Cocktail Counterpoint" . . . . . GEORGES, DINDON, MME. DINDON, JACOB

"The Best of Times". . . . . ALBIN, JACQUELINE, PATRONS

"Tell Her I'm Happy". . . . . .NELSON

"Look Over There" reprise . . . . JEAN-MICHEL

"Finale". . . . . COMPANY

AUTHOR'S NOTES

"This is all about love, this marriage," says Albin to Georges when he hears of their son's impending marriage. And it's what I say to you when describing not only the creation of this musical comedy, but the collaboration that brought *La Cage aux Folles* into being.

From the moment that Jerry Herman, Arthur Laurents and I began work, in the summer of '82, ours has been a marriage of love, respect and trust. We (the "Collaborationists," as we call ourselves) worked hand in hand in hand, almost single-mindedly, adapting the long-running French play for the musical stage.

*La Cage...*in its original form was a bevy of sight gags, wildly drawn characters and sexual rompery. Truly the fabric of farce. What was lacking for our creative team was the stuffing–the helium that would fill our beautiful bejewelled balloon and make it soar. That stuffing was the heart. Without that heart Jerry could not make it sing and I could not make it speak. It took many long hours of discussion to find the heart of our piece. In our incarnation *La Cage...* is a love story, the tale of a marriage of 20 years almost ruined by a son's thoughtlessness.

Here, amidst the age-old triangle of mother, father and child, we found our justification, our universality, our reason to create. What child has not at some point in its life been ashamed to introduce its parents to friends? What parent has not wondered, "Where did we go wrong?" What marriage has not been tested in these familial flames? When Georges asks his son what had the boy ever asked for that he'd been refused, Jean-Michel answers, "A little respect for what I want, a little understanding." Georges, taken aback, answers, "A *little* respect? A *little* understanding?" and, referring to Albin, sings, "How often is someone concerned with the tiniest thread of your life? ...Look over there!" Now we had our stuffing!

Adding to our music, lyrics and libretto the elements of costume, scenery, lighting and dance was more than adding icing on the cake. We were blessed with the genius of Theoni Aldredge, David Mitchell, Jules Fisher and Scott Salmon. Each element added new levels to our creation, new heights and flavors and spicings. The scenery placed us in the fantasy world of St. Tropez, all sun-bleached pastels and sparkling blue Mediterranean waters. The costumes gave us character, glamour and style. The lighting added mood of moonlit nights, starry skies and romance. The choreography gave us life exploding before our very eyes. Here was fun, boundless energy and humor. And last but hardly least, our hats are off to Allan Carr, Barry Brown, Fritz Holt and our other producers for their vision and faith.

To say that *La Cage...* is a unique creation, only time will tell. But I can say that its birth was unique. We "Collaborationists" love one another deeply and want nothing more than to share that love with you. Our only wish, as Georges would say, is that you "Open your eyes! For if we've done our job correctly, you will leave with more than a torn ticket stub and a folded program." Messieurs-dames, we give you *La Cage aux Folles.*

– Harvey Fierstein, *for the Collaborationists*

ACT ONE

SCENE 1

*(***GEORGES** *appears downstage center and addresses the audience.)*

[MUSIC NO. 00: **PROLOGUE**]

GEORGES. *Bon soir! Bon soir!* What pleasure it gives me to say, *Bon soir!* Here we are at the pride of St. Tropez, the envy of the cabaret world, the jewel of the Riviera. What legend has told and rumour has promised we shall do our utmost to deliver. *(waving and winking)* Ah, so many old friends. And so many new faces. And so many old friends with new faces. But we can linger no longer–the inevitable is upon us–*Messieurs-dames*, I welcome you to the fifteenth edition of our world famous revue starring the one and only Zaza, and featuring the notorious and dangerous *Cagelles!*

(timpani roll)

Ladies and Gentlemen and…you, we issue the following warning: Please remain in your seats while *Les Cagelles* perform. The management cannot be responsible for your safety. And now, I beg you…open your eyes. You have arrived at *La Cage Aux Folles!!!*

[MUSIC NO. 2: **WE ARE WHAT WE ARE**]

(Curtain rises to reveal "Les Cagelles", a chorus line of beautiful drag performers.)

CAGELLES. *(men only)*
WE ARE WHAT WE ARE
AND WHAT WE ARE
IS AN ILLUSION

13

WE LOVE HOW IT FEELS
PUTTING ON HEELS
CAUSING CONFUSION

WE FACE LIFE
THO IT'S SOMETIMES SWEET AND SOMETIMES BITTER
FACE LIFE
WITH A LITTLE GUTS AND LOTS OF GLITTER
LOOK UNDER OUR FROCKS
GIRDLES AND JOCKS
PROVING WE ARE WHAT WE ARE
WE ARE WHAT WE ARE

WOMEN.

HALF A BRASSIERE

MEN.

HALF A SUSPENDER

ALL.

HALF REAL AND HALF FLUFF
YOU'LL FIND IT TOUGH
GUESSING OUR GENDER
SO JUST *(whistle)*
IF WE PLEASE YOU THAT'S THE WAY TO SHOW US
JUST *(whistle)*
CAUSE YOU'LL LOVE US ONCE YOU GET TO KNOW US
LOOK UNDER OUR GLITZ
MUSCLES AND TITS
PROVING WE ARE WHAT WE ARE

(The "PARADE:" they all promenade.)

(After the "PARADE," GEORGES steps forward to present the featured performers.)

GEORGES. For your delight, I present the songbird of Avignon, the nightingale of Nice, the triller from Manila. When she opens her throat, the swallows return to Capistrano in shame. Permit me to present: Chantal!

*(**CHANTAL** sings a coloratura run and exits.)*

*(**GEORGES** introduces his next Cagelle.)*

Merci, Chantal. And now, turn your attention to a darker hue, Hanna from Hamburg!

Men call her diva.

Women call her devil.

Police call her daily!

(**HANNA** *performs with a bullwhip.* **GEORGES** *takes back the stage.*)

Danke Hanna.

And lastly, Phaedra the enigma.

All the fortunes of the pharaohs, the riches of Rangoon, the babble of Babylon cannot pry loose the secret of her fatal charm.

(**PHAEDRA** *sticks her tongue out and exits.*)

(**GEORGES** *takes back the stage.*)

Thank you Phaedra. And now on with the extravaganza!

(*Les Cagelles return in bathing outfits.*)

CHANTAL. Auntie Em, Auntie Em.

(*2 CAGELLE tap*)

(*beach ball section*)

MERCEDES. Hi boys!

CHANTAL. AHHH!

(*Beach balls are kicked into the audience.*)

CAGELLES.

WE...
FACE LIFE
THO IT'S SOMETIMES SWEET AND SOMETIMES BITTER
FACE LIFE
WITH A LITTLE GUTS AND LOTS OF GLITTER
LOOK UNDER OUR FROCKS
GIRDLES AND JOCKS
PROVING WE ARE WHAT WE ARE

(*Cannons, on a military ship set piece, explode.*)

*[MUSIC NO. 2A **Introducing Zaza**]*

CAGELLES.

> WE FACE LIFE
> THO IT'S SOMETIMES SWEET AND SOMETIMES BITTER
> FACE LIFE
> WITH A LITTLE GUTS AND LOTS OF GLITTER
> HANG ONTO YOUR WIG
> AND GIVE A BIG WELCOME TO ZAZA OUR STAR

(They present Zaza's entrance. Nothing happens.)

(Cagelles turn to face upstage and repeat their intro.)

> HANG ONTO YOUR WIG
> AND GIVE A BIG WELCOME TO ZAZA OUR STAR

*(The curtain falls and the **CAGELLES** fall to the floor.)*

*(**FRANCIS**, the stage manager, has entered with his clipboard and headset, shouting at the **GIRLS**. He has a small band-aid on his temple.)*

FRANCIS. Get back on, get back on. Zaza isn't here yet. You've got to give them an encore.

BITELLE. Phaedra's feet hurt.

FRANCIS. Phaedra's ass is gonna hurt; get back on stage!

*(**BABETTE** enters with basket.)*

BABETTE. Wigs. Wigs.

FRANCIS. No. They have to do it again. Zaza's still in her room. Shoo.

CHANTAL. If she's late, why do I have to suffer?

PHAEDRA. You want to be a woman? Learn to suffer.

*(**HANNA** sidles up to **FRANCIS** seductively.)*

HANNA. And you must learn to suffer?

FRANCIS. If I can't get Zaza to the stage…

BITELLE. Will we get overtime?

CHANTAL. Only Zaza gets overtime.

PHAEDRA. Zaza *is* overtime!

(GEORGES enters and crosses to bang on the dressing room door.)

GEORGES. Albin! Albin! Please let me in.

HANNA. Step away from the door, Georges. Leave this to a professional. *(HANNA cracks her whip.)* Zaza! Come!!!!

GEORGES. Francis, would you please get her back on the stage!

FRANCIS. Hanna doesn't take orders well.

HANNA. But I give them brilliantly.

GEORGES. How about this: You do the encore this instant or tomorrow night you appear as a man.

HANNA. You wouldn't dare!

GEORGES. Francis, inform wardrobe. I'm sure they can find a pair of trousers large enough to fit Herman.

(HANNA storms out and FRANCIS follows…)

GEORGES. *(catching FRANCIS)* Francis! Be careful.

(FRANCIS shrugs and retreats.)

VOICE. *(off stage)* Prepare the way! *J'approche!*

GEORGES. Albin, at last!

(The dressing room door opens and out steps JACOB in full feather drag.)

JACOB. Dim the lights, cue my music, and start the applause. I am ready.

GEORGES. And just what do you think you are doing in one of Zaza's gowns?

JACOB. Madame Zaza's appearance has been delayed due to circumstances beyond earthly control. And so, as my mistress is indisposed, I feel it my duty as her friend, confidante, and personal handmaiden to be certain that the show go on.

GEORGES. An applaudable sentiment, Jacob. But this season we are not featuring butlers in the revue.

JACOB. I am no one's butler. I am the maid!

GEORGES. I hired a butler.

JACOB. And you got a maid!

(JACOB *starts to exit –* GEORGES *returns to dressing room door…*)

GEORGES. *(bangs on door)* Albin, I will count to three and then, so help me, I will…have someone break down this door!

JACOB. Very forceful. And I'm certain my mistress would be shaking in her boots if she could hear you. But Madame is in repose above.

GEORGES. Above?

JACOB. Upstairs.

*[MUSIC NO. 2B: **INTO THE APARTMENT**]*

(JACOB *reveals the apartment and exits.*)

GEORGES. Thank you; very clever.

SCENE 2

GEORGES. Albin! Albin!!

ALBIN. *(offstage)* Who dares to call my name, I who have been so wronged?

GEORGES. What are you doing in the kitchen?

ALBIN. Wrestling with a casserole that wouldn't come clean!

GEORGES. Albin, you are going to drive me mad. Do you have any idea what time it is? Hurry and get dressed.

ALBIN. Where were you this afternoon?

GEORGES. What's the difference? Get dressed!

ALBIN. I made a magnificent luncheon. You said you'd be home. You weren't.

GEORGES. See how she listens to me.

ALBIN. I de-boned a chicken, stuffed her with wild rice and pistachios, anointed her with apricot glaze and topped her off in truffles and where were you? In *absentia!*

GEORGES. There are two hundred paying customers waiting for HER, and HE'S reciting the luncheon menu.

ALBIN. It's not the chicken, Georges. It's the thought behind the chicken.

GEORGES. The thought behind the what????

(**JACOB** *appears from behind a drape.*)

JACOB. The thought behind the chicken. *(off* **GEORGES**' *leer)* Did I say that out loud? *Pardonnez-moi.*

GEORGES. *(to* **JACOB***)* Don't you have something else to do?

JACOB. Many things.

GEORGES. Then do them!

ALBIN. Don't yell at my maid.

GEORGES. She's not your maid. She's your butler.

JACOB. Now I ask you.

(**JACOB** *exits as* **FRANCIS** *enters.*)

FRANCIS. Mercedes is on. You're next, Zaza.

ALBIN. They'll wait. We're speaking.

(**FRANCIS** *retreats.*)

GEORGES. They will not wait, get dressed!

(**ALBIN** *holds out two gold bracelets.*)

What now?

ALBIN. Ankle bracelets, if you please.

GEORGES. If you didn't wear that iron lung of a corset you could bend down and put them on yourself.

ALBIN. You used to love putting on my ankle bracelets.

GEORGES. There is a difference between loving to and having to.

ALBIN. And so we have it. The beans are at last spilt. The cat is out the baggage. Feeling trapped, my love? Is this what twenty years together adds up to? Where once knelt a prisoner of love, now crouches a caged creature longing to be free.

GEORGES. We're in fine form tonight. Brava, Zaza.

ALBIN. Oh, it's all painfully clear. First you start missing meals, then my ankle bracelets, and then...bunk beds.

GEORGES. Could I stop you now if I begged?

ALBIN. I can already see the final blow: Some boney, brunette boy, draped across my chaise, popping bonbons, puffing pot, making a mockery of our marriage vows. It's all my fault for falling in love with a younger man.

GEORGES. Darling, please. I'm only eight years younger.

ALBIN. Five years.

GEORGES. Actually, sixteen.

ALBIN. Alright, eight.

GEORGES. Albin, you know there's no one else but you.

ALBIN. Pity me. Betray me. But don't lie to me Georges. How could I have been so blind? For months I've watched my roles dwindle down. Where once I was your inspiration, your muse, I am now reduced to naught but comic relief.

GEORGES. Oh, I see where this is headed. Forget it!

ALBIN. Forget what?

GEORGES. You want me to drag out that old warhorse production of *Salome* again, don't you? Well, you can forget it.

ALBIN. Who said anything about *Salome*? I'm talking about... *(The actress emerges.)* And just what is wrong with my *Salome*?

GEORGES. And away we go.

ALBIN. Audiences adored my *Salome*. I'll have you know that when I finished the dance of the Seven Veils and raised the head of John the Baptist to my lips, the audiences cried out, tears in their eyes, handkerchiefs stuffed in their mouths.

GEORGES. But darling, audiences prefer laughing without stuffing handkerchiefs in their mouths. Albin, Albin my love, there comes a time in every Salome's life when she can no longer risk dropping the last veil.

*(**FRANCIS** appears in the door again.)*

FRANCIS. Are you coming? Mercedes is on her last verse. For the fourth time!

ALBIN. And apparently so am I!

*(**FRANCIS** exits.)*

Jacob, pack my gowns. We leave at sunrise!

GEORGES. Albin, the show...?

ALBIN. The show will go on. And so shall I. *Solo. Perdutto. Abandonatta.* Like a dog on a rock.

GEORGES. Like a what? On a what?

*(**JACOB** enters.)*

JACOB. Like a dog on a rock. Pardon.

GEORGES. All right. I give in. You win, my Albin, you win. You shall play *Salome* again next season. Now–get dressed. Please.

*[MUSIC NO. 3: **MASCARA**]*

(**ALBIN** *nods.* **GEORGES** *blows him a kiss and backs out of the room.*)

(**ALBIN** *takes off slippers and head scarf and sits at his dressing table.*)

ALBIN. And so I've won. What have I won? Zaza gets to play Salome, and Albin eats alone. *(looking in mirror)*
ONCE AGAIN I'M A LITTLE DEPRESSED
BY THE TIRED OLD FACE THAT I SEE–

(spin mirror)

ONCE AGAIN IT IS TIME TO BE SOMEONE
WHO'S ANYONE OTHER THAN ME–
WITH A RARE COMBINATION
OF GIRLISH EXCITEMENT AND MANLY RESTRAINT–

(checking brushes)

I POSITION MY PRECIOUS ASSORTMENT
OF POWDERS AND PENCILS AND PAINT–
SO WHENEVER I FEEL THAT MY PLACE IN THE WORLD
IS BEGINNING TO CRASH

I APPLY ONE GREAT STROKE OF MASCARA
TO MY RATHER LIMP UPPER LASH!

(He does so.)

AND I CAN COPE AGAIN!

(He does a 2nd lash and looks front.)

GOOD GOD! THERE'S HOPE AGAIN!

(He puts down mascara.)

WHEN LIFE IS A REAL BITCH AGAIN

AND MY OLD SENSE OF HUMOUR HAS UP AND GONE

IT'S TIME FOR THE BIG SWITCH AGAIN
I PUT A LITTLE MORE MASCARA ON...

WHEN I COUNT MY CROWS FEET AGAIN

AND TIRE OF THIS PERPETUAL MARATHON
I PUT DOWN THE JOHN SEAT AGAIN
AND PUT A LITTLE MORE MASCARA ON...

AND EVERYTHING'S SPARKLE DUST
BUGLE BEADS
OSTRICH PLUMES

WHEN IT'S A BEADED LASH THAT YOU LOOK THROUGH

CAUSE WHEN I FEEL GLAMOROUS AND
ELEGANT AND
BEAUTIFUL
THE WORLD THAT I'M LOOKING AT'S BEAUTIFUL TOO!

WHEN MY LITTLE ROAD HAS A FEW BUMPS AGAIN
AND I NEED SOMETHING LEVEL TO LEAN UPON
I PUT ON MY SLING PUMPS AGAIN
AND WHAM–THIS UGLY DUCKLING IS A SWAN!

SO WHEN MY SPIRITS START TO SAG
I HUSTLE OUT MY HIGHEST DRAG
AND PUT A LITTLE MORE MASCARA ON...

AND EVERYTHING'S
ANKLE STRAPS
MARIBOU
SHALIMAR
IT'S WORTH SUCKING IN MY GUT...GIRDLING MY REAR

'CAUSE EVERYTHING'S RAVISHING

(wig on)

SENSUAL
FABULOUS
WHEN ALBIN IS TUCKED AWAY
AND ZAZA IS HERE!

(**ALBIN** *crosses downstage and is suddenly Zaza in the club.*)

Come to Mama...
WHEN EVERYTHING SLIDES DOWN THE OLD TUBES AGAIN
AND WHEN MY SELF-ESTEEM HAS BEGUN TO DRIFT

> I STRAP ON MY FAKE BOOBS AGAIN
> AND LITERALLY GIVE MYSELF A LIFT
> SO WHEN IT'S COLD AND WHEN IT'S BLEAK
> I SIMPLY ROUGE THE OTHER CHEEK

(The **CAGELLES** *appear.)*

ALBIN. *(cont.)*

> FOR I CAN FACE ANOTHER DAY
> IN SLIPPER SATIN LINGERIE
> TO MAKE DEPRESSION DISAPPEAR
> I SCREW SOME RHINESTONES ON MY EAR
> AND PUT MY BROOCHES AND TIARA
> AND A LITTLE MORE MASCARA

ALBIN.	**6 CAGELLES.**
ON...	SPARKLE DUST
	BUGLE BEADS
ANKLE STRAPS	ANKLE STRAPS
MARIBOU	MARIBOU
ON...	OSTRICH PLUMES
	SHALIMAR
	RAVISHING
ON!!!	ON!!!

*[MUSIC NO. 3A: **MASCARA ENCORE**]*

6 CAGELLES.

> SPARKLE DUST
> BUGLE BEADS
> ANKLE STRAPS
> MARIBOU
> OSTRICH PLUMES
> SHALIMAR
> RAVISHING
> FABULOUS

*(***ALBIN*** returns in a new wig.)*

ALBIN. My hair may be black, but my roots are blonde.

> AND EVERYTHING'S
> ANKLE STRAPS
> MARIBOU

SHALIMAR
IT'S WORTH SUCKING IN MY GUT AND GIRDLING MY REAR
'CAUSE EVERYTHING'S RAVISHING
SENSUAL
FABULOUS
WHEN ALBIN IS TUCKED AWAY AND ZAZA IS HERE!

(transform back into the living room)

SCENE 3A

(The Living Room)

(The music can still be heard faintly from offstage as **GEORGES** *enters from the club.)*

GEORGES. *(checking his watch)* Only seven minutes late. Not bad for the first show.

*(*JACOB *enters from the kitchen now dressed in trenchcoat, dark glasses and hat as a lady spy.)*

Ah, the return of the very pink panther.

JACOB. Be nice or I will run as fast as these feet (mules) will carry and tell my mistress all about the "special visitor" stashed in the kitchen.

GEORGES. *(excitedly)* You don't mean…he's here?

JACOB. Oh, he's here, all right.

*(*GEORGES *tries to rush to the kitchen but* JACOB *blocks his way.)*

Not so quick, Slick. Before I let you see him we will reiterate our bargain.

GEORGES. *(gritting his teeth)* Go on.

JACOB. I will keep my mouth shut about you-know-who being up here while keeping Albin away down there.

GEORGES. And in return?

JACOB. You put me in the show.

GEORGES. For one number.

JACOB. Agreed.

GEORGES. In the chorus.

JACOB. They haven't built the chorus strong enough to hold me!

GEORGES. Go. See to Albin.

JACOB. Yes, my collaborationist. *(*JACOB *gives a secret knock on the kitchen door.) (secretively through the door)* Attention! The manly moose mainly moons Mongolians! Carry on!

(and adjusting his spy collar, off **JACOB** *flies)*

GEORGES. Well, at least he's not on drugs.

[MUSIC NO. 3B: JEAN MICHEL'S ENTRANCE]

(A handsome young man enters with a wine bottle in hand. He sees **GEORGES** *and opens his mouth, but* **GEORGES** *halts him…)*

Mon Coeur. At last you have returned to me. No. Don't say a word. Let me simply drink you in.

JEAN-MICHEL. Wouldn't you rather have a glass of wine?

GEORGES. How wonderful you look. And how I've ached to see that smile. A month without you seemed an eternity.

JEAN-MICHEL. I've missed you too. And Albin…?

GEORGES. Safely tucked away. We have hours to ourselves. Come and give me a kiss.

*(***JEAN-MICHEL*** takes* **GEORGES** *up in warm embrace, kissing both cheeks.)*

My love. My life. My heaven.

JEAN-MICHEL. Oh, Papa. Can we save the dramatics for when Albin gets back?

*(***JACOB*** reappears through the club door carrying Zaza's gown. He is now dressed as a maid.)*

JACOB. *Comment marveilleux!* At last our son is home!

GEORGES. OUR son? And are you supposed to be watching Albin?

JACOB. Do I tell you how to do your job?

JEAN-MICHEL. Papa, let him be. I must say I like the outfit.

JACOB. Just a little something to serve your every need.

ZIS FOR ME,
ZAT FOR YOU,
AND ZIS FOR YOUR PAPA!

*(***JACOB*** finishes with a big bump towards* **GEORGES** *and flees the room, as* **JEAN-MICHEL** *laughs.)*

GEORGES. Stop! You're encouraging him.

JEAN-MICHEL. He only behaves that way because he loves you.

GEORGES. If he loved me he'd vacuum!

JEAN-MICHEL. God, it's good to be home.

GEORGES. No more holidays for you. I can't bear the stress.

JEAN-MICHEL. I won't be here long, Papa. I'm getting married.

GEORGES. You know, this is what I love about you. You have something to say, you say it. No hemming. No hawing. Clear, precise, and right to the point. Like a knife in the heart.

JEAN-MICHEL. I was going to send a telegram.

GEORGES. What? And miss the pleasure of seeing your father die before your eyes? Nonsense.

JEAN-MICHEL. And I was worried you wouldn't take it well.

GEORGES. You could be right.

JEAN-MICHEL. You mean you're not pleased for me?

GEORGES. Not that I noticed. But perhaps I'm working up to it. And who is it you're marrying? Not that Veronique!

JEAN-MICHEL. Her name is Anne, Papa.

GEORGES. Don't change the subject. You go off on holiday with this Antoinette and she coerces a proposal out of you. It's ridiculous. You're twenty years old, Jean-Michel. Much too young to engage with any Annisette.

JEAN-MICHEL. Her name is Anne. And I'm twenty-four.

GEORGES. Are you sure?

JEAN-MICHEL. Sit down, Papa. I have a little problem.

GEORGES. Twenty-four? So have I.

JEAN-MICHEL. The problem is Anne's parents. Her father is Dindon…Edouard Dindon…Deputy General of the T.F.M.

GEORGES. You know me and politics darling. What is the T.F.M?

JEAN-MICHEL. The Tradition, Family, and Morality Party.

GEORGES. Ooh, I like the sound of that. There's a little something in there for everybody.

JEAN-MICHEL. But it's not terribly compatible with La Cage Aux Folles.

GEORGES. And why not? We have Tradition. And who loves their family more than we? And Morale is an area in which we certainly don't stint. And a Deputy in the family. We can use a little political clout these days, what with that fanatic running for office. You know the one who's pledged to close down all the transvestite clubs if elected.

(*JACOB re-enters to collect an iron, and just in time for…*)

JEAN-MICHEL. His name is Dindon.

JACOB & JEAN-MICHEL. Edouard Dindon.

JACOB & JEAN-MICHEL & GEORGES. Deputy General of the T.F.M.

JEAN-MICHEL. And he's coming to meet you.

GEORGES. You're insane.

JEAN-MICHEL. He, his wife, and Anne will be staying overnight.

GEORGES. Probably certifiable.

JEAN-MICHEL. They'll arrive for cocktails tomorrow.

GEORGES. And we'll all come see you at the asylum. Why would you want to marry into a family like that?

JEAN-MICHEL. Anne is nothing like her father, so there's nothing to worry about.

GEORGES. Except her father!

JEAN-MICHEL. We'd better get to work. We should start by toning this place down a little. You know, ditch a few of the more obvious ironies in the décor.

GEORGES. And while you're ditching the ironies, what's to become of me?

JEAN-MICHEL. I took the liberty of telling them you were with the French Foreign Service. Retired, of course. Don't worry. I was very vague.

GEORGES. Well, if you can't be truthful, be vague.

JEAN-MICHEL. We'll use the house entrance, and we'll close off that door to the club.

GEORGES. And just who will Albin be? French attaché to Finnochio's?

JEAN-MICHEL. Anything he'd like as long as he isn't here.

(a moment)

Papa, you know the way he is. The way he talks and moves and...dresses. You know.

GEORGES. So, it's a farewell to Albin! Just like that. The man raises you as his own for the last twenty years and suddenly you turn 'round and say, "I'm engaged to the daughter of a fanatic. So, "Zis is for her, Zat for you, and Zilch for your papa!" Judas!

JEAN-MICHEL. Papa!

GEORGES. Traitor!

JEAN-MICHEL. Papa, please...

GEORGES. Heterosexual!

JEAN-MICHEL. Papa, there's no one like Anne. I'd do anything for her.

GEORGES. Nonsense. You've been in love a dozen times.

JEAN-MICHEL. Not like this.

GEORGES. No? What about Paulette? Helene?

JEAN-MICHEL. No one. Never like this.

GEORGES. She's bewitched you!

JEAN-MICHEL. Entirely.

*[MUSIC NO. 4: **WITH ANNE ON MY ARM**]*

GIRLS HAVE COME AND GONE, PAPA
ANGELIQUE AND ANTOINETTE
WHO DID I PREFER?
LESLIE OR HELENE?
IT WAS ALL A BLUR AND YET, PAPA
WHEN ANNE COMES RUNNING DOWN THE STREET
AND I LINK MY ARM IN HERS

GIRLS HAVE COME AND GONE
GIRLS MAY COME AND GO

BUT SOMETHING VERY ODD OCCURS, PAPA
'CAUSE
LIFE IS IN PERFECT ORDER
WITH ANNE ON MY ARM
IT MAKES MY SHOULDERS BROADER
WITH ANNE ON MY ARM
EVEN WHEN THINGS WON'T JELL
AND THE PIECES WON'T FIT
I'M SUDDENLY IN
I'M SUDDENLY ON
I'M SUDDENLY IT!

WHO ELSE CAN MAKE ME FEEL
LIKE I'M HANDSOME AND TALL
WHO ELSE CAN MAKE ME FEEL
I'M ON TOP OF IT ALL
I FOUND A COMBINATION
THAT WORKS LIKE A CHARM
I'M SIMPLY A MAN
WHO WALKS ON THE STARS
WHENEVER IT'S ANNE ON MY ARM

(**JACOB** and **JEAN-MICHEL** *dance.*)

JEAN-MICHEL.   **GEORGES.**

LIFE IS A CELEBRATION
WITH ANNE ON MY ARM

                                                SINCE GIRLS AND SEX ARE
                                                  HIS CREDO

WALKING'S A NEW
   SENSATION
WITH ANNE ON MY ARM

                                                THANK GOD HE'S GOT MY
                                                  LIBIDO

EACH TIME I FACE A
   MORNING
THAT'S BORING AND
   BLAND

JEAN-MICHEL. *(cont.)*	GEORGES. *(cont.)*
WITH HER IT LOOKS GOOD	
	HE'S FANNING ANOTHER FLAME
	HIS RHETORIC IS THE SAME
IT'S GRAND	
	IT'S ONLY THE NAME THAT CHANGES
SOMEHOW SHE'S PUT A PERMANENT STAR IN MY EYE	
	BUT AFTER ALL, HE'S A GREAT KID
EVEN THE DEAD OF WINTER CAN FEEL LIKE JULY	
	SO FULL OF CHARM FOR A STRAIGHT KID
WE START A CONFLAGRATION THAT'S CAUSE FOR ALARM WE'RE GIVING OFF SPARKS	
	IF THERE'S A CHANCE THEY'LL BE JUST LIKE ALBIN AND ME THEN MAYBE IT'S ANNE
THEN MAYBE IT'S ANNE	
	THEN MAYBE IT'S ANNE
THEN MAYBE IT'S ANNE	

(**JACOB** *magically transforms into* **ANNE.**)

(**JEAN-MICHEL** *and* **ANNE** *dance.*)

(orchestra)

(**JEAN-MICHEL** *whirls* **ANNE** *around the room and finally spins her off the stage.*)

JEAN-MICHEL.
WHO ELSE CAN MAKE ME FEEL
LIKE I'M HANDSOME AND TALL

WHO ELSE CAN MAKE ME FEEL
I'M ON TOP OF IT ALL
I FOUND A COMBINATION
THAT WORKS LIKE A CHARM
I'M SIMPLY A MAN
WHO WALKS ON THE STARS
WHENEVER IT'S ANNE ON MY ARM

GEORGES. You make a most convincing case.

JEAN-MICHEL. One more thing…

GEORGES. Please, no more things.

JEAN-MICHEL. The Dindons are coming to meet my parents.

GEORGES. So you've said.

JEAN-MICHEL. I'd like to invite Mother.

GEORGES. Mother who?

JEAN-MICHEL. Mother Sybil. My mother.

GEORGES. You haven't seen her in decades. Why would you want to invite her?

JEAN-MICHEL. Because the Dindons want to meet my parents.

GEORGES. So?

JEAN-MICHEL. That usually involves a father and a mother.

GEORGES. So?

JEAN-MICHEL. So Sybil's my mother.

GEORGES. So?

JEAN-MICHEL. So would you please call and invite her?

(**GEORGES** *pauses non-plussed.*)

I love you.

GEORGES. You had better.

(*They embrace.*)

Now, just who breaks all of this wonderful news to Albin?

(**ALBIN** *enters.*)

ALBIN. Wedding bells? Is someone tolling wedding bells?!?!?!?

GEORGES. Jacob strikes again!

ALBIN. What have we raised, Georges, an animal? Snakes live male and female together. Cats live male and female together. We are human beings. We know better. Child, child, child. You are a boy, she is a girl. What would you talk about?

GEORGES. There's no reasoning with him when he's like this. Run.

JEAN-MICHEL. I love her, Albin.

ALBIN. I love women too, but I wouldn't marry one. Oh, Georges, we're losing our only child. And I shall have no more.

GEORGES. Not without a miracle.

ALBIN. *(to* **JEAN-MICHEL***)* Look how thin you are. It's that girl!

JEAN-MICHEL. You always say I'm too thin.

ALBIN. Just march yourself into the kitchen and have Jacob warm some soup.

JEAN-MICHEL. Albin…

ALBIN. You're not a married man yet. Now march!

GEORGES. *(to* **JEAN-MICHEL***)* I'll talk to him.

JEAN-MICHEL. Albin, I'm sorry.

(He exits.)

ALBIN. He's sorry. He's sorry. Oh, Georges, our baby is getting married. Where did we go wrong?

GEORGES. We've been through worse my love. We'll get through this. We still have an hour before the next show. How about some fresh air?

ALBIN. I'm too upset. I couldn't possibly be seen in public.

*[MUSIC NO. 5: **WITH YOU ON MY ARM**]*

GEORGES. With me you could.

LIFE IS A CELEBRATION
WITH YOU ON MY ARM

ALBIN. I'm too upset.

GEORGES. That's because you're not listening.

ALBIN. I am listening. I'm always listening.

GEORGES.

> LIFE IS A CELEBRATION
> WITH YOU ON MY ARM
> IT'S WORTH THE AGGRAVATION
> WITH YOU ON MY ARM

ALBIN. Well, he always did bounce back quicker.

GEORGES. That's because I'm more limber.

ALBIN. You always were.

GEORGES.

> EACH TIME I FACE A MORNING
> THAT'S BORING AND BLAND
> WITH YOU IT LOOKS GOOD.

ALBIN. You can't dance.

GEORGES. With you I can.

> WITH YOU IT LOOKS GREAT

ALBIN. Do I have to?

GEORGES. Yes.

> WITH YOU IT LOOKS GRAND!

> *(***GEORGES*** *and* **ALBIN** *dance.)*

ALBIN. Like the old days!

GEORGES. *(executing a fancy step)* Uh huh.

ALBIN. *(imitating him)* Uh huh.

GEORGES. *(another step)* Uh huh.

ALBIN. *(imitating him again)* Uh huh.

GEORGES. *(now an especially complex step)* Uh huh.

ALBIN. *(giving up)* Unh-unh.

> ON YOU IT LOOKS GOOD

> *(***ALBIN*** *watches* **GEORGES** *soft-shoe.)*

> ON YOU IT LOOKS GREAT...

> *(the same)*

> ON YOU IT LOOKS GRAND...

BOTH. *(stepping together)*
SOMEHOW YOU'VE PUT A PERMANENT
STAR IN MY EYE
EVEN THE DEAD OF WINTER
CAN FEEL LIKE JULY
I FOUND A COMBINATION
THAT WORKS LIKE A CHARM

*(**ALBIN** is suddenly on the end of the chaise, stuck in mid air. **GEORGES** lifts him off.)*

GEORGES.
IT'S SUDDENLY…

*(blows a kiss to **ALBIN**)*

ALBIN.
IT'S SUDDENLY

(sighs)

BOTH.
WHENEVER IT'S YOU

WHENEVER IT'S YOU

WHENEVER IT'S YOU ON
WHENEVER IT'S YOU ON
WHENEVER IT'S YOU…
ON…
MY…
ARM….!

*[MUSIC NO. 5A: **PLAYOFF**]*

SCENE 4

*[MUSIC NO. 7: **PROMENADE**]*

(The Promenade)

*(**RENAUD** and **MME. RENAUD** set the café as **JEAN-MICHEL** waits anxiously on the corner.)*

*(**COLETTE** and **ETIENNE** approach…)*

RENAUD. *Bonsoir.*

JEAN-MICHEL. *Bonsoir.*

COLETTE. Well, Jean-Michel!

JEAN-MICHEL. Hello Colette.

COLETTE. You know my friend Etienne?

JEAN-MICHEL. Nice to meet you, Etienne.

*(**ETIENNE** eyes **JEAN-MICHEL** warily.)*

COLETTE. Jean-Michel is my cousin, Etienne.

ETIENNE. You have a lot of cousins.

COLETTE. Family is family. *(on the sly to **JEAN-MICHEL**)* Give me an hour to ditch him and I'll meet you at La Cage.

JEAN-MICHEL. It's all right, Etienne, I won't be in town long. Colette, I'm getting married.

COLETTE. Congratulations. Give me half an hour.

*(Music swells as **COLETTE** and **ETIENNE** exit. **ANNE** enters.)*

ANNE. Jean-Michel! Sorry I'm late.

(They kiss.)

How did it go with your parents?

JEAN-MICHEL. Oh, they're thrilled for us. They can't wait to meet you. How about yours?

ANNE. My mother's happy. But my father is so busy lecturing the world on how to run their families that he has no idea what's going on with his own. Oh, Jean-Michel, you're so lucky to have normal parents.

JEAN-MICHEL. Well, I'm not sure how normal any par...

(*JEAN-MICHEL freezes.* **ALBIN** *and* **GEORGES** *enter. His mouth hangs open...*)

ANNE. Jean-Michel, what's wrong?

JEAN-MICHEL. What say we take a walk on the beach?

ANNE. Are you reading my mind?

JEAN-MICHEL. Let's go.

ANNE. But the beach is that way.

JEAN-MICHEL. It's starting to rain. We'd better run for cover.

ANNE. What?

JEAN-MICHEL. I just felt a drop.

ANNE. Jean-Michel, the sky couldn't be clearer.

(*He grabs her and kisses her.*)

JEAN-MICHEL. It's starting to rain. (*kiss*) Anne, if you love me you'll believe me. (*kisses her again*) It's starting to rain. (*kiss*)

(*JEAN-MICHEL starts to exit,* **ANNE** *pulls him to her and kisses him.*)

ANNE. And so it is.

(*They run off.* **ALBIN** *and* **GEORGES** *move downstage.*)

GEORGES. Feeling any better, my love?

ALBIN. A *bit.* And yet the world appears so dark and gloomy.

GEORGES. It's nighttime and you're wearing sunglasses.

(**TABARRO** *enters.*)

(**GEORGES** *and* **ALBIN** *sit at a café table.*)

TABARRO THE FISHERMAN. *Bon soir, messieurs.*

GEORGES & ALBIN. *Bon soir, messieur.*

TABARRO. The fish are running well.

ALBIN. Jacob will be by in the morning.

TABARRO. *Merci. Au revoir.*

GEORGES & ALBIN. *Au revoir.*

ALBIN. Oh, Georges, our nest is on empty.

GEORGES. An ineludible fact of life my love; you can't keep children in cages.

ALBIN. *(considering this)* Well, not forever.

(**COLETTE** *and* **ETIENNE** *enter.*)

GEORGES. *Bon soir*, Etienne.

ETIENNE. *Bon soir…*

GEORGES. *Bon soir..?*

COLETTE. Colette.

COLETTE & ETIENNE. *Bon Soir.*

GEORGES. Oh please.

(**COLETTE** *and* **ETIENNE** *exit.*)

ALBIN. It seems like only yesterday Jean-Michel bounced on his mama's knee.

GEORGES. Speaking of mamas, there's something we need…

(**JACQUELINE,** *a stylish and imposing woman carrying flowers, enters.*)

JACQUELINE. *Cher* Georges! *Cher* Albin!

GEORGES & ALBIN. *Cher* Jacqueline!

JACQUELINE. How opportune! I have just sent a party of very important patrons from my restaurant down to your little club. Midnight show. Ringside table?

GEORGES. Of course.

JACQUELINE. Problem, *mon doux?*

GEORGES. No, not for you. I'll send them champagne.

JACQUELINE. *Merci.*

ALBIN. And I'll send you the bill.

JACQUELINE. Oh, Albin, you little jokester! *Mille fois!*

(*She exits with a flourish.*)

RENAUD. *Bienvenue. Mes cher amis.*

GEORGES. The usual.

MME. RENAUD. *(appearing with two brandies) Voila!*

ALBIN. And how are the children?

Get-een-g   Bee-gar

RENAUD. Getting bigger.

MME. RENAUD. Growing older.

ALBIN. Aren't we all, *n'est pas?*

MME. RENAUD. *Oui, tu parle...*

> (**MME. RENAUD** *goes into the café,* **RENAUD** *sits in the café entrance and reads.*)

GEORGES. While we're on the subject...

ALBIN. What subject?

GEORGES. Mothers. You know that Anne's parents are coming to meet Jean-Michel's family and I thought it would be nice if he had his mother there with him.

ALBIN. Well of course I'll be there. Where else would I be?

GEORGES. Not you, Albin. Sybil.

ALBIN. *(pause)* Sybil who?

GEORGES. Sybil. Jean-Michel's mother.

ALBIN. By "Sybil. Jean-Michel's mother" do you refer to that British tart who seduced you one night backstage at the Lido in Paris? That Welsh rarebit who once, every three or four years, thinks to send her own flesh and blood son a birthday card? Always, I might add, on her birthday and not his? Is that the English muffin to whom you refer?

GEORGES. That's the one.

ALBIN. Georges, without threats or tantrums I tell you now; if that woman comes, you die.

GEORGES. If only it were that easy.

ALBIN. What right has she to butt into the boy's life now? Where has she been all these years when he was growing up and actually needed his mother? I'll tell you where: huddled in every corner of the world, in any corner of the room with any kind of man she could lay her claws on, that's where she's been. When I think of the times he called her, he wrote her, he begged her to come and always the same reply: "So sorry, son, some other time." Oh, I could bat the bitch!

GEORGES. Nevertheless, she *is* his mother. She did carry him for nine months.

ALBIN. I'd have delivered in eight. And not to your doorstep!

GEORGES. Nevertheless, I have called her and she is coming.

ALBIN. And what else? I know your face when you're holding back. You might as well give me all the bad news at once. Who else have you invited to this soiree?

GEORGES. It's not the invited that's bothering me.

ALBIN. *Excusez-moi?*

GEORGES. Tonight of all nights there has to be a full moon.

ALBIN. Beautiful, isn't it?

   [MUSIC NO. 8 : SONG ON THE SAND]

GEORGES. And you had to wear that cologne.

ALBIN. Don't you like it?

GEORGES. Like it? And on top you had to wear that particular shade of blue.

ALBIN. But it's your favourite.

GEORGES. I know. I know. Oh, Albin...

   (**GEORGES** *goes to touch* **ALBIN**'s *shoulder.*)

ALBIN. *(pulling away)* Georges, please. We're in public view.

GEORGES. I must be insane. To think that after all these years you can still bring a blush to my cheek.

ALBIN. You old fool.

GEORGES.
   DO YOU RECALL
   THAT WINDY LITTLE BEACH WE WALKED ALONG?
   THAT AFTERNOON IN FALL
   THAT AFTERNOON WE MET
   A FELLOW WITH A CONCERTINA SANG...
   WHAT WAS THE SONG?
   IT'S STRANGE WHAT WE RECALL
   AND ODD WHAT WE FORGET...

I HEARD LA DA DA DA DA DA DA
AS WE WALKED ON THE SAND
I HEARD LA DA DA DA...
I BELIEVE IT WAS EARLY SEPTEMBER
THROUGH THE CRASH OF THE WAVES
I COULD TELL THAT THE WORDS WERE ROMANTIC
SOMETHING ABOUT SHARING
SOMETHING ABOUT ALWAYS

THOUGH THE YEARS RACE ALONG
I STILL THINK OF OUR SONG ON THE SAND
AND I STILL TRY AND SEARCH
FOR THE WORDS I CAN BARELY REMEMBER
THOUGH THE TIME TUMBLES BY
THERE IS ONE THING I AM FOREVER
CERTAIN OF
I HEAR LA DA DA DA DA DA DA
DA DA DA DA DA DA
AND I'M YOUNG AND IN LOVE

(Musical interlude; they turn to each other; **GEORGES**
reaches for **ALBIN**'s hand, he moves away...)*

...I BELIEVE IT WAS EARLY SEPTEMBER
THROUGH THE CRASH OF THE WAVES
I COULD TELL THAT THE WORDS WERE ROMANTIC
SOMETHING ABOUT SHARING

*(***GEORGES**' *fingers creep across the table.)*

SOMETHING ABOUT ALWAYS

*(***ALBIN**'s *fingers do the same.)*

THOUGH THE YEARS *(their fingers link)* RACE ALONG
I STILL THINK OF OUR SONG ON THE SAND
AND I STILL TRY AND SEARCH
FOR THE WORDS I CAN BARELY REMEMBER
THOUGH THE TIME TUMBLES BY
THERE IS ONE THING I AM FOREVER
CERTAIN OF
I HEAR LA DA DA DA DA DA DA
DA DA DA DA DA DA
AND I'M YOUNG AND IN LOVE

ALBIN. *(with a romantic sigh, as the music continues)* Oh, Georges, you play my heart like a concertina. You're such a poet. I'm not so sure about "the crash of the waves", this being the Mediterranean. But basically you are correct. This is all about love, this wedding. Not jealousies or old wounds. So, Sybil can come. And the three of us will bear witness to our son's marriage together. Hand in hand...in hand.

GEORGES. Albin, there's something more you should know...

(a clock chimes)

ALBIN. *(rising)* Oh, Georges. We'll be late for the second show.

GEORGES. Wait. Albin! I need to tell you something.

ALBIN. *(stopping and turning)* Later, *cherie*. I mustn't keep my audience waiting.

(He exits.)

GEORGES. Tonight for the first time in his life he has to be on time. Oh, Albin, you're still a surprise.

(sings)

I HEAR LA DA DA DA DA DA DA
DA DA DA DA DA DA
AND I'M YOUNG AND IN LOVE

(GEORGES *exits.)*

*[MUSIC NO. 8A: **SONG ON THE SAND – PLAYOFF**]*

*(The **RENAUDS** clear the café as the stage transforms into backstage, with **LES CAGELLES** in various stages of readiness for the show.)*

SCENE 5

(The club wings)

*(They stretch and warm up as **FRANCIS**, with a clipboard in hand and wearing a neck brace, tries to make announcements.)*

CHANTAL. *(sotto) (offering some take away to **BITELLE**)* You want a little?

BITELLE. *(sotto)* Oh, no thank you, dear. I ate last week.

FRANCIS. Tomorrow's schedule has a brush-up rehearsal for the tap number at four. And at five I want to see everyone involved in last night's Dragon Dance disaster. How many times do I have to tell you: The flames are meant to come out of the dragon's *mouth!*

*(The **GIRLS** all laugh.)*

(checking his notes) Jacob will be taking the collection for Jean-Michel's wedding gift.

MERCEDES. Oh, what are we giving him?

CHANTAL. We could bake a cake.

BITELLE. And I could come out of it.

MERCEDES. I could make a ratatouille!

HANNA. Rat-tat-touille?

*(**MERCEDES** performs Rat-tat-touille to the tune of La Cucaracha. They all join in.)*

FRANCIS. Five minutes! Five minutes to the top of the show.

*(No one listens or moves. **FRANCIS** throws his hands up in frustration. **GEORGES** enters.)*

GEORGES. Here are my lovelies. Happily laughing the night away while my business goes down the drainpipes.

*(**HANNA** steps forward.)*

HANNA. Leave them to me. All right, Ladies. Move it or lose it!

(HANNA cracks her whip, and LES CAGELLES exit. HANNA advances on FRANCIS.)

GEORGES. Practicing, Hanna?

HANNA. Making perfect.

GEORGES. *(looking at the brace)* What's been happening to you?

FRANCIS. I'm dating Hanna.

(HANNA cracks her whip and points offstage and FRANCIS rushes off, followed by HANNA.)

GEORGES. *(to himself)* Could I make this a rest home?

(JEAN-MICHEL enters through the stage door.)

JEAN-MICHEL. I've got a van outside to put it all in.

GEORGES. Put all what in?

JEAN-MICHEL. All the things from the apartment.

GEORGES. Are you planning on moving something?

JEAN-MICHEL. Just the statues, the paintings, some furniture...

GEORGES. Some furniture?

JEAN-MICHEL. I guess we can start in Albin's closets.

GEORGES. Start what in Albin's closets? Surely these people are not going to conduct searches of our closets?

JEAN-MICHEL. Where will Mother put her clothes?

GEORGES. She can leave them in the taxi for all I care.

JEAN-MICHEL. But how will it look if she doesn't sleep in your room?

GEORGES. Like any couple married twenty years.

(FRANCIS appears and salutes militarily to GEORGES.)

FRANCIS. *Herr Kapitan,* we await your order to attack. *(clicks his heels)*

GEORGES. Alert the orchestra. I'll get Zaza.

(FRANCIS goes off.)

JEAN-MICHEL. Papa, I'd like to get this settled now...

(**ALBIN** *appears from the apartment in a bathrobe.* **JEAN-MICHEL** *turns away.*)

(**GEORGES** *crosses to* **ALBIN**.)

GEORGES. Ah, look at my Zaza. A vision in terry cloth. You take my breath away.

ALBIN. Thank you, Georges. *(crossing to* **JEAN-MICHEL**) Jean-Michel, I thought after the show you, your father and I might share a bit of supper and discuss the wedding plans. Doesn't that sound delightful?

JEAN-MICHEL. *(exiting)* Absolutely. I'll be up in the apartment working on your room.

ALBIN. Working on my room?

GEORGES. Spring cleaning. Swatting the cobwebs and lassoing the dust bunnies.

ALBIN. But why spring clean when it isn't spring?

GEORGES. It will be. One day. With any luck.

(**FRANCIS** *enters again.*)

FRANCIS. I've got an audience, an orchestra, and a song to sing. All we need now is a star.

ALBIN. Fear not, sweet Saint Francis, your star is on the rise. Jacob, Jacob, lips! *Mes enfants... j'approche!!!*

(**JACOB** *applies* **ALBIN**'s *lipstick and* **ALBIN** *exits to the stage.*)

FRANCIS. Places, everyone. Places.

(**FRANCIS** *follows* **ALBIN** *off.* **JACOB** *exits into the dressing room.*)

JEAN-MICHEL. I'm sorry. I thought you'd told him.

GEORGES. You've a lesson to learn in your young life: Discretion is the better part of marriage.

JEAN-MICHEL. Come on. Let's go. There's lots to do.

GEORGES. Just one minute. Come here. I want to make sure you know what you're asking me to do. Look at him. The man who has dedicated the last twenty years to making a home for us. Who has lived almost exclusively for our comfort. Yours and mine. I want you to look at him and consider what it is you're doing; throwing him out of the home he has made for us...

JEAN-MICHEL. For one night. Please. *(a moment)* I am only doing what's necessary.

SCENE 5A

*[MUSIC NO. 8B: **BEFORE LA CAGE**]*

(The stage transforms into the club.)

*(**GEORGES** greets his guest and with a gesture starts a drum roll.)*

GEORGES. Midnight. It makes you even more attractive. You know why you're here, and so do I. It's time for our midnight show! What legend has told and rumour has promised, we will do our utmost to deliver. And now the moment you have long awaited; La Cage Aux Folles proudly presents the greatest star on the Riviera–the one, the only Zaza!!!!

*(Music note: ZaZa's entrance occurs at measure 35 of 8B: **BEFORE LA CAGE**.)*

ALBIN. Good evening. Good evening. Bon soir, one and all. Are you having fun? Give me a moment, I'm just getting started.

(bump and rimshot)

Shall we try that again?

(bump and rimshot)

I hope our staff has made you comfortable. *(eyeing someone in the house)* Perhaps not *that* comfortable! Did you all get enough to drink? Obviously you did.

Don't you look decorative? Have you ever pictured yourself on the arm of an older woman? Let me rephrase that. On the arm of a rich, older woman? Write down your number, I will give it to my mother.

(eyeing that person again) So you've all come to see our little show, have you? Well, that you shall. For those of you who have wandered in off the street unbeknownst... I am Zaza!

ORCHESTRA. Hi, Zaza!!!

ALBIN. Hello boys! (They are so needy) And for those of you who couldn't guess from our tastefully appointed signage outside, this is La Cage Aux Folles

[MUSIC NO. 9: LA CAGE AUX FOLLES]

Here at La Cage we live life–how should I put it?–on an angle. Ok, when I say that, can you all lean slightly that way? On an angle…! There are some people in the cheap seats not sure which way they go. Shall we try again? On an angle. Stop, stop, There is a man down here trying to go both ways! Not to worry. You'll soon get your bearings. Take a deep breath, open your eyes. What do you see?

(She sings…)

IT'S RATHER GAUDY
BUT IT'S ALSO RATHER GRAND
AND WHILE THE WAITER PADS YOUR CHECK
HE'LL KISS YOUR HAND
THE CLEVER GIGOLOS
ROMANCE THE WEALTHY MATRONS
AT LA CAGE AUX FOLLES

IT'S SLIGHTLY FORTIES, AND A LITTLE BIT "NEW WAVE"
YOU MAY BE DANCING WITH A GIRL WHO NEEDS A SHAVE
WHERE BOTH THE RIFFRAFF
AND THE ROYALTY ARE PATRONS
AT LA CAGE AUX FOLLES

LA CAGE AUX FOLLES
THE MAITRE D' IS DASHING
CAGE AUX FOLLES
THE HATCHECK GIRL IS FLASHING
WE IMPORT THE DRINKS THAT YOU BUY
SO YOUR PERRIER IS CANADA DRY!

ECCENTRIC COUPLES ALWAYS PUNCTUATE THE SCENE
A PAIR OF EUNUCHS AND A NUN WITH A MARINE
TO FEEL ALIVE YOU
GET A LIMOUSINE TO DRIVE YOU
TO LA CAGE AUX FOLLES

JACQUELINE.

IT'S BAD AND BEAUTIFUL; IT'S BAWDY AND BIZARRE.

ALBIN.

I KNOW A DUCHESS WHO GOT PREGNANT AT THE BAR!

JACQUELINE & ALBIN.

JUST WHO IS WHO

ALBIN & JACQUELINE.

AND WHAT IS WHAT
IS QUITE A QUESTION

JACQUELINE.

AT LA CAGE AUX FOLLES
GO FOR THE MYSTERY, THE MAGIC AND THE MOOD

*(**ALBIN** pushes **JACQUELINE** back into her seat.)*

AVOID THE HUSTLERS

ALBIN.

AND THE MEN'S ROOM

FRANCIS.

AND THE FOOD

ALBIN.

FOR YOU GET GLAMOUR
AND ROMANCE

JACQUELINE.

AND INDIGESTION

ALBIN & JACQUELINE.

AT LA CAGE AUX FOLLES

ALL.

LA CAGE AUX FOLLES

ALBIN.

A ST. TROPEZ TRADITION

ALL.

CAGE AUX FOLLES

ALBIN.

YOU'LL LOSE EACH INHIBITION
ALL WEEK LONG WE'RE WONDERING WHO
LEFT A GREEN GIVENCHY GOWN IN THE LOO

ALL.

YOU GO ALONE TO HAVE THE EVENING OF YOUR LIFE

ALBIN.

YOU MEET YOUR MISTRESS AND YOUR BOYFRIEND AND
YOUR WIFE

ALL.

IT'S A BONANZA;

IT'S A MAD EXTRAVAGANZA

AT LA CAGE AUX FOLLES

(The curtain is raised to reveal a birdcage full of **LES
CAGELLES** *as dazzling birds.)*

(BIRDS SECTION:)

(Pole dance)

(Creatures)

(Table dancing)

(Ballet)

(Pairs cooing)

(The **BIRDS** *exit.)*

*(***ALBIN** *reappears in a huge white fur and blonde wig.)*

ALBIN. Did you miss me? You could hardly expect me to
stay out here with those girls leaping and flying and
flailing in that manner. *(to that patron again)* Hello.
Have you ever seen legs go up so high or so fast? Well,
I'm sure you have. In the mirror!

(modelling the dress) While I was backstage, I took the
opportunity to slip into a little something...else. This
is something else, isn't it!

(eyeing someone in the audience) Hello darling. Oh, I
know why you got seats so close to the stage. Hoping to
peek at all our little secrets aren't you? Well, I will tell
you something confidentially...

Among my girls there are no *little* secrets!

(trumpet: wah, wah, wah)

ALBIN. *(cont.)* Ah, I see we have a new trumpet player. Does your mother know what your lips do for a living?

(wah, wah, wah)

But does she know what they will do for me after the show?

(siren music)

(**ALBIN** *is suddenly Marlene Dietrich.*)

Hello, this is a little song I sang in the war. I sang it in Paris. I sang it in Berlin. I sang it in Sicily. I sang it till they made me stop. It is about a soldier. He meet a girl and fall in love. He give her his heart. She look at it and give it back. I sing it for you now.

YOU'LL BE SO DAZZLED BY THE AMBIENCE YOU'RE IN
YOU'LL NEVER NOTICE THAT THERE'S WATER IN THE GIN.
COME FOR A DRINK...
AND YOU MAY WANNA SPEND THE WINTER
AT LA CAGE AUX FOLLES

LA CAGE AUX FOLLES
A ST. TROPEZ TRADITION
CAGE AUX FOLLES
YOU'LL LOSE EACH INHIBITION

WE INDULGE EACH CHANGE IN YOUR MOOD
COME AND SIP YOUR DUBONNET IN THE NUDE

Come on girls!

(The curtain rises to reveal a Moulin Rouge set piece and **LES CAGELLES** *appear for the cancan:)*

(Yeow!)

(Wheel)

(Solo kicks)

(Bitelle's acro)

(Legs)

(Solos section)

(Pairs spinning)

CAGELLES.

> LA LA LA
> LA LA LA LA LA LA LA
> LA LA LA
> LA LA LA LA LA LA LA
>
> LA LA LA LA LA LA LA LA
> LA LA LA LA LA LA LA LA LA LA
>
> *(Splits #1)*
>
> *(Splits #2)*
>
> *(Snap heads to audience)*
>
> *(Button)*
>
> *(Number restarts.)*
>
> (**ALBIN** *appears in the centre of the cancan line*)

CAGELLES.

> LA LA LA
> LA LA LA LA LA LA LA
> LA LA LA
> LA LA LA LA LA LA LA
>
> LA LA LA LA LA LA LA LA
> LA LA LA LA LA LA LA LA LA LA

ALBIN.

> COME AND ALLOW YOURSELF TO LOSE YOUR SELF
>   CONTROL
> COME AND INVESTIGATE THE DARK SIDE OF YOUR SOUL
> COME FOR A GLIMPSE AND YOU MAY WANNA STAY FOREVER
>   AT
> LA CAGE AUX FOLLES

ALL.

> YOU CROSS THE THRESHOLD AND YOUR BIRDGES HAVE
>   BEEN BURNED
> THE BAR IS CHEERING FOR THE DUCHESS HAS RETURNED
> THE MOOD'S CONTAGIOUS
> YOU CAN BRING YOUR WHOLE OUTRAGEOUS ENTOURAGE
> (OUTRAGEOUS ENTOURAGE)

(OUTRAGEOUS ENTOURAGE)
OUTRAGEOUS ENTOURAGE!
IT'S HOT AND HECTIC
EFFERVESCENT AND ECLECTIC
AT LA CAGE AUX FO............LLES!

(**ALBIN** *comes center stage, removes his wig and curtsies deeply.*)

(*The stage transforms into backstage.*)

SCENE 6

*[MUSIC NO. 10: **HANNA'S INTRO**]*

*[MUSIC NO. 10A: **HANNA'S TANGO**]*

*(**CAGELLES** frantically change **HANNA** into dominatrix costume, and **ANGELIQUE** into a leopard.)*

*(**FRANCIS**, standing before a microphone, hand over his ear in best voice-over tradition…)*

BITELLE. Sweet Jesus, take me now!

FRANCIS. Ladies and Gentlemen, the management of La Cage Aux Folles continuously scours the globe to bring you the fiercest in entertainment. And now, from the deepest corner of your darkest fantasies…the eternal struggle of man versus beast…the apocryphal battle of beauty versus leather…tanned, tawed and tenderised…HANNA FROM HAMBURG!

(A loud crack of the whip and a scream!)

*(**ALBIN** is changing for his next number behind a dressing screen.)*

*(**GEORGES** and **JEAN-MICHEL**, carrying a large nude statue and some clothing, are spotted heading from the apartment toward the exit.)*

GEORGES. All clear.

ALBIN. *(exclaiming in French:)* Attention! *(in English)* Spring cleaning is one thing, but where are you going with my gowns?

GEORGES. Go change, I'll explain it all later.

ALBIN. Explanations are being entertained now, if you please.

JEAN-MICHEL. Would you tell him?

FRANCIS. Two minutes, Zaza.

GEORGES. Finish changing. Everything's fine.

ALBIN. No, everything is not fine.

FRANCIS. Keep it down, ladies. There's an artist at work here.

(**HANNA** *cracks her whip "onstage."*)

ALBIN. Georges. I'm waiting.

JEAN-MICHEL. Papa, please. Tell him.

GEORGES. All right, Albin. I shall explain it all. And I'm certain that if I tell you quietly and calmly we can discuss this like two mature adults.

ALBIN. (*crossing behind the screen*) It's that bad.

GEORGES. Not really. You know that Anne's parents are coming. And I told you that Sybil is coming. What I failed to tell you is that you're not. You know that politician who's trying to impose his morality on the coast? Well, he is the girl's father. So, what can you do? You can't choose your parents. But Jean-Michel assures me that Anne is nothing like her father. So, let us be thankful for small favours. Meanwhile, they are who they are and they're on their way here. And so, for one night, I shall be someone else for them. And for that night Sybil will be my wife.

And after they've gone we'll have a good laugh at how we pulled one over on them. When you think about it, it's all very funny; me a diplomat with the French Foreign Service, Sybil, my wife, and you...believe me, this will be one of those stories we'll laugh about for years to come. So, what do you say?

(**ALBIN** *appears from behind the screen fully dressed to go onstage. He looks at* **GEORGES** *and* **JEAN-MICHEL**, *but says nothing.*)

JEAN-MICHEL. I'm sorry, Albin.

(**GEORGES** *begins to move towards* **ALBIN**.)

ALBIN. Excuse me. I have a show to finish.

(**ALBIN** *crosses to center stage as the stage with* **LES CAGELLES** *in position is revealed.*)

(**GEORGES** *and* **JEAN-MICHEL** *exit.*)

SCENE 6A

*[MUSIC NO. 11: **I AM WHAT I AM**]*

ALBIN & CAGELLES.
WE ARE WHAT WE ARE
AND WHAT WE ARE
IS AN ILLUSION
WE LOVE HOW IT FEELS
PUTTING ON HEELS
CAUSING CONFUSION
WE FACE LIFE
THO IT'S SOMETIMES SWEET AND SOMETIMES BITTER...

*(But he cannot go through it and suddenly holds up his hands for the **COMPANY**, for the orchestra, for **EVERYBODY** to stop:)*

ALBIN. No! Please, please.

CAGELLES. *(fading)*
...FACE LIFE
WITH A LITTLE GUTS

ALBIN. *(quieter, to the **COMPANY**)* Get off.

*(**ALL** exit. **ALBIN** stands alone, and after a long moment, starts to sing a capella:)*

I AM WHAT I AM
I AM MY OWN SPECIAL CREATION...
SO COME TAKE A LOOK
GIVE ME THE HOOK
OR THE OVATION.

IT'S MY WORLD
THAT I WANT TO HAVE A LITTLE PRIDE IN
MY WORLD
AND IT'S NOT A PLACE I HAVE TO HIDE IN
LIFE'S NOT WORTH A DAMN
TILL YOU CAN SAY "HEY, WORLD
I AM WHAT I AM!"

I AM WHAT I AM
I DON'T WANT PRAISE

I DON'T WANT PITY
I BANG MY OWN DRUM
SOME THINK IT'S NOISE
I THINK IT'S PRETTY
AND SO WHAT
IF I LOVE EACH FEATHER AND EACH SPANGLE?
WHY NOT
TRY AND SEE THINGS FROM A DIFFERENT ANGLE?
YOUR LIFE IS A SHAM
TILL YOU CAN SHOUT–OUT LOUD
"I AM WHAT I AM!"

I AM WHAT I AM
AND WHAT I AM
NEEDS NO EXCUSES
I DEAL MY OWN DECK
SOMETIMES THE ACE
SOMETIMES THE DEUCES
THERE'S ONE LIFE
AND THERE'S NO RETURN AND NO DEPOSIT
ONE LIFE
SO IT'S TIME TO OPEN UP YOUR CLOSET
LIFE'S NOT WORTH A DAMN
TILL YOU CAN SAY–"HEY, WORLD
I AM…
WHAT…
I AM!"

(**GEORGES** *steps from the wings toward him.*)

(**ALBIN** *turns and freezes* **GEORGES** *with his determined glare.* **ALBIN** *thrusts his wig to* **GEORGES** *and walks triumphantly off the stage, into the house and straight out of the theatre.*)

(**GEORGES** *is left alone, aghast.*)

(*The curtain falls.*)

ACT TWO

SCENE 1

(Town and Café)

*(Thunder. A funeral dirge plays. **ALBIN** enters wearing a black pants suit and sunglasses. **JACOB** follows in makeshift Greek tragic robes, holding a parasol over **ALBIN**.)*

*(**GEORGES** enters from the café.)*

GEORGES. Albin, I've been worried sick. I searched all night for you.

JACOB. Please to keep your distance. Have you no respect for a homeless widow wandering the earth, ill-fated, ill-starred and ill-dressed?

ALBIN. *(to **JACOB**)* You said you liked this outfit.

JACOB. It was better on Liza.

*(**GEORGES** shoves **JACOB** aside to get to **ALBIN**. **ALBIN** ducks away behind the protective parasol.)*

GEORGES. Albin, please, I need to talk to you.

JACOB. A traitor's needs are but specks of sand tossed into the hurricane of humiliation.

*(Again **GEORGES** pushes **JACOB** aside but still can't reach **ALBIN** beyond the parasol.)*

GEORGES. Where did you sleep? Have you eaten? You look exhausted.

JACOB. The Gods watch o'er their woeful child, oh, Jason!

GEORGES. Listen, Medea, I've got fifty francs say you've got someplace else to be.

JACOB. As if my loyalty could be bought for fifty francs. You make me laugh. Ha, ha!!!

GEORGES. What would you say to a hundred?

(Holds out cash. **JACOB** *trades it for the parasol.)*

JACOB. I'd say, just in time. My arms are killing me. *(to* **ALBIN***)* I take my leave, Mistress. Even the devotion of thy faithful servant cannot shield thee from the whizzing arrows of destiny. But I'll pick up lunch and meet you back at the house. Okay?

(exiting while counting the money)

Later!

*(***JACOB** *gone,* **GEORGES** *approaches* **ALBIN***.)*

GEORGES. Albin, my love…

ALBIN. I have nothing to say to you, Georges.

GEORGES. I'm sorry. All right?

ALBIN. No, I'm sorry, it is NOT all right. To think I would live to see the day when Jean-Michel, who I raised as my own, would turn his back on me…

GEORGES. And didn't you lie to your parents about me?

ALBIN. But I had to lie. They would never have accepted that you were…in show business.

GEORGES. Jean-Michel is a kid. He wasn't thinking. He's in love.

*[MUSIC NO. 12B: **SONG ON THE SAND – REPRISE**]*

ALBIN. And you?

GEORGES. I'm just a fool. Who also wasn't thinking. Who's also in love.

ALBIN. *(hearing the music)* How much do you pay him/her?

GEORGES.

THROUGH THE… *SPLASH* OF THE WAVES
I COULD TELL THAT THE WORDS WERE ROMANTIC
SOMETHING ABOUT SHARING

ALBIN.

SOMETHING ABOUT ALWAYS

(**GEORGES** *and* **ALBIN** *begin to move together, but stop as they see* **TABARRO** *enter.*)

GEORGES & ALBIN.

THOUGH THE YEARS RACE ALONG
I STILL THINK OF OUR SONG ON THE SAND
AND I STILL TRY AND SEARCH
FOR THE WORDS I CAN BARELY REMEMBER
THOUGH THE TIME TUMBLES BY
THERE IS ONE THING THAT I AM FOREVER
CERTAIN OF

GEORGES.

I HEAR LA DA DA DA DA DA DA...

ALBIN.

...LA DA DA DA DA DA DA
DA DA DA DA DA DA

GEORGES & ALBIN.

AND I'M YOUNG AND IN LOVE!

(**GEORGES** *moves to* **ALBIN**, *but* **ALBIN** *puts up his hand to hold him off.*)

ALBIN. The fact remains that I am unwanted.

GEORGES. Albin, you are wanted. It's all you bring with you that's questionable. Now, you have certain mannerisms, albeit charming mannerisms, which could shock people who haven't been forewarned.

ALBIN. *Et tu?* (*mocking him*) "Which could shock people who haven't been forewarned!"

GEORGES. My mannerisms can translate as tasteful affectation. While yours are no less than suspicious.

ALBIN. "No less than sssssusssssspiciousssssssss."

(**RENAUD** *enters from the café.*)

RENAUD. *Bonjour, mes amis.* Breakfast?

ALBIN. No!

GEORGES. Yes.

(**RENAUD** *returns to the café.*)

ALBIN. You can eat while I suffer?

GEORGES. I'll force myself.

ALBIN. Pig.

GEORGES. Albin, the point is if you wish to attend tonight's affair you can do so simply by donning the proper attire and appropriately straightening up your act. You will assume the role of Jean-Michel's dear Uncle Al.

ALBIN. Uncle Al!?!?!

GEORGES. What's the matter with that?

ALBIN. The displacement in stature for one thing! Even if you had a wife who was a drunk, you wouldn't pass her off as a maid.

GEORGES. Ah, but a drunken wife is at least a woman. And in the minds of the masses a lush is more presentable than a fruit.

ALBIN. And suddenly you're no fruit? Just because you had a baby one night by accident.

GEORGES. It was no accident.

ALBIN. You told me it was an accident.

GEORGES. I said no such thing. Sybil was the most beautiful showgirl at the Lido...

ALBIN. Sybil's a pig.

GEORGES. I shall ignore that remark. Sybil was the most beautiful showgirl at the Lido and I, playing a Greek God, was certainly pound for pound her match. The opportunity presented herself and I thought, "Why not? Everybody talks about it so much. I might as well see what the fuss is all about." And it was a beautiful and moving experience.

ALBIN. As if you could remember, drunk as you were.

GEORGES. I lasted from midnight till quarter to three. How drunk could I have been?

ALBIN. That's right. Smack me in the face with your infidelities. Animal!

GEORGES. Albin, are you coming tonight or not?

ALBIN. As Uncle Al?

GEORGES. As Uncle Al. Please.

ALBIN. All right. I'll come as Uncle Al...bert. But only because, whether he knows it or not, the boy needs me. Besides, without me there, you're bound to screw things up.

GEORGES. Thank you, my love. Now to prepare. Up up up. Slouch!

ALBIN. Slouch?

GEORGES. Go ahead. Slouch!

(**ALBIN** *tries.*)

Perhaps a standing slouch is too advanced. Lets try slouching in that chair.

(**RENAUD** *appears with a breakfast tray an̓ ⸱⸱ː it on the table.*)

(**ALBIN** *sits in a chair at the table.*)

He's going to pass as a heterosexual man tonight. It will be the greatest acting challenge of his career. *(sharply to* **ALBIN***)* SLOUCH!

(**ALBIN** *screams.*)

What's the matter?

ALBIN. You yelled at me.

MME. RENAUD. What?

ALBIN. I'm sorry, he yelled at me.

[*MUSIC NO. 12C:* ***MOUNTAIN BUILD*** *(musical accompaniment)*]

GEORGES. Yes, I yelled at you. But you're all man. You must face up to your destiny. Even if it means being yelled at. You must say to yourself, "Something untoward has happened to me. I have been yelled upon. But I am all man! I am strong! I am invincible! I will climb back up that mountain!!!"

(**GEORGES** *cuts off the orchestra with a flourish.* **ALBIN** *jumps to his feet.*)

ALBIN. Bravo! Bravo, mon heros!

(**GEORGES** *ushers* **ALBIN** *back to the seat.*)

GEORGES. And now you–drop your shoulders. Let them go all round and beaten. Stop holding in your stomach. Let it spill out over your lap, a testament to all the nights out drinking with the boys. Now spread your legs.

ALBIN. *Excusez-moi?*

GEORGES. You're wearing trousers, not a skirt. Spread them!

(**ALBIN** *inches his feet apart while keeping his knees together.*)

Ahem…

(**ALBIN** *parts his legs and quickly closes them again.*)

Now pick up that croissant.

(*He does, notices its shape and mimes suggestive activities.*)

Not like that. Like a he-man. Let's try the toast. Think of…

RENAUD. John Wayne!

[MUSIC NO. 13: **MASCULINITY**]

GEORGES. Perfect! John Wayne. I want you to pick up that toast as if you were John Wayne.

(**ALBIN** *prepares, does his best gunslinger swagger, then sits back down and lifts the toast, fanning himself with it.*)

I thought I said John Wayne.

ALBIN. It is John Wayne. John Wayne as a little girl!

GEORGES. Let's try this again.

THINK OF THIS AS…
MASCULINE TOAST

AND MASCULINE BUTTER
READY FOR SPREADING BY A MASCULINE HAND
PICK UP THAT KNIFE AND MAKE BELIEVE IT'S A MACHETE
IT'LL TAKE ALL YOUR STRENGTH AND STEADY NERVES
FOR HACKING YOUR WAY THROUGH THE CHERRY
    PRESERVES!
THINK OF JOHN WAYNE   *Salute*
AND JEAN-PAUL BELMONDO
THINK OF THE LEGIONNAIRES AND CHARLEMAGNE'S MEN
SO LIKE A STEVEDORE YOU GRAB YOUR CUP
AND IF, GOD FORBID, THAT YOUR PINKY POPS UP
YOU CAN CLIMB BACK UP THE MOUNTAIN ONCE AGAIN!
You got that?

ALBIN. I think so.

GEORGES. Don't think. Know! You're a man.

ALBIN. I'm a man. *Step forward*

RENAUD. You're a man. *X*

ALBIN. I'm a man.

MME. RENAUD. You're a man.

ALBIN. Does anyone hear an echo?

MME. RENAUD. Oh, Albin!

    (**MME. RENAUD** *tickles* **ALBIN** *playfully and he screams.*)

GEORGES. That's great. (Now, about that voice of yours.)
    GRUNT LIKE AN APE
    AND GROWL LIKE A TIGER
    GIVE US THAT ROARING, SNORING, MASCULINE LAUGH

ALBIN. *(falsetto)* HA!

GEORGES.
    ALWAYS REMEMBER THAT JOHN WAYNE WAS NOT SOPRANO
    KEEP MAKING IT ROUGH, AND GRUFF, AND LOW

ALBIN.
    HO HO

GEORGES.
    TRY MORE LIKE JOHN WAYNE AND LESS BRIGITTE BARDOT!

RENAUD. *DS Right*
    THINK OF DE GAULLE

AND THINK OF RASPUTIN

MME. RENAUD.

THINK LIKE A DANIEL MARCHING INTO THE DEN

GEORGES.

WHILE TRYING TO JOIN THE BURLY BRUTES

IF YOU FORGET THAT YOUR NYLONS ARE UNDER YOUR
      BOOTS

GEORGES, RENAUD & MME. RENAUD.

YOU CAN CLIMB BACK UP THE MOUNTAIN ONCE AGAIN!

GEORGES. Now try to imitate my walk.

(**GEORGES** *walks with questionable machismo.*)

ALBIN. I can't do that…I'll put my back out!

RENAUD. Watch me.

MME. RENAUD. No, no, no. Watch me.

(*She walks in an easy male style.*)

GEORGES. Yes. You see how she holds herself? Shoulders
back, hips planted.

ALBIN. It's easy for her. She's wearing flats.

GEORGES. Just feel it, right?

RENAUD. Right!

TABARRO. Right!

GEORGES. Albin, you are the greatest performer on the
Riviera. You've done the likes of Shakespeare, Moliere,
and came this close to getting that tour of Dolly. Are
you telling me that playing dear simple Uncle Al is
beyond your range?

(*The gauntlet has now been thrown.* **ALBIN** *stands and
steps centre of the group.*)

ALBIN. Stand back!

(*And with that* **ALBIN** *launches into his own masculine
march. The* **OTHERS** *join in.*)

ALL.

THINK GHENGIS KHAN

AND THINK TARAS BULBA

THINK OF ATTILA'S HUNS AND ROBIN HOOD'S MEN
TRY NOT TO WEAKEN OR COLLAPSE
IF THEY DISCOVER THE PANTY-HOSE UNDER YOUR CHAPS
YOU CAN CLIMB BACK UP THE MOUNTAIN ONCE AGAIN!
WHOA...YEAH!

(play off)

(ALBIN, GEORGES, RENAUD, *and* **MME. RENAUD** *exit.)*

SCENE 2

(The lights come up on the apartment. It is now stripped bare but for a huge wooden crucifix upstage right and a few pieces of dark wooden furniture.)

*(*JACOB *enters dressed as Louis Quinze footman in brocade and powdered wig. The doorbell chimes.)*

[MUSIC NO. 13A and 13B: **MASCULINITY PLAYOFF** *and* **JACOB'S CROSS***]*

*(*JACOB *opens the door to reveal* JEAN-MICHEL.*)*

JACOB. Ah, the prodigal son.

JEAN-MICHEL. *(entering with a large tray)* I picked up the *hors d'oeuvres.*

JACOB. Thank you. I'm starving.

JEAN-MICHEL. Has Mother arrived yet?

JACOB. Mother who?

JEAN-MICHEL. Don't you think that outfit smacks a bit of overkill?

JACOB. No more than your decorating.

JEAN-MICHEL. Do you think I went too far?

JACOB. When it comes to going too far, you're asking the wrong person.

JEAN-MICHEL. You'd better behave tonight. Father, you and I have made a deal.

JACOB. And so we did. For twenty-one hours I perform to the full perfection of my butler best, and in return, tomorrow night, when the curtains of La Cage rise – they rise on ME!

JEAN-MICHEL. In the chorus!

JACOB. Featuring ME!

JEAN-MICHEL. Just for the finale.

JACOB. What more do ME need? Theatrical legend will recall the moment when a single lavender spot revealed this quinceañera goddess adrift in a cloud of perfumed mist, draped from comely crown to flawless foot in leopard lame. Men will reach out to me in longing. Women will avert their envious eyes. And you will have to speak to my agent, 'cause if you think I'm going to keep dusting and vacuuming this mess once I have been discovered you got another thing coming!

(JACOB *slaps himself down in a chair with a "humph."*)

(GEORGES *enters dressed in a tasteful suit.*)

GEORGES. Ah! Mother Theresa's decorator has returned.

JEAN-MICHEL. I suppose that suit will do. You are, after all, supposed to be retired.

GEORGES. If that's a compliment, I accept.

JEAN-MICHEL. I'm sorry. You look very handsome.

GEORGES. I know. Wait until you see Albin.

JEAN-MICHEL. Albin?

JACOB. *(crossing himself)* Oh yes. Albin.

GEORGES. Oh, but it's fun to be on the other side of shocking news. Yes, Albin! We've been rehearsing all afternoon. This will be the crowning moment of his long illustrious career. Tonight, the great Zaza as "Uncle Albert."

JEAN-MICHEL. God save us all.

GEORGES. Albert! Oh, Uncle Albert! Come forth and show our son the Frankenstein his love hath wrought.

(ALBIN *appears in a blue suit and black flats. Nervous, his hands rest uncomfortably in his pockets.*)

Voila! A fellow to be reckoned with. Your Uncle Albert.

(JEAN-MICHEL *looks aghast.* ALBIN *looks worried, but* GEORGES *encourages him to come forward.*)

(ALBIN *moves tentatively.*)

(ALBIN *decides this is all too much and makes a dash for the door.* GEORGES *retrieves him and ushers him towards* JEAN-MICHEL.)

ALBIN. It's not working.

GEORGES. *Veni. Veni.* You're doing splendidly. Handsome. Dashing. You'll soon have women mobbing you in the streets. And not just for make-up tips.

(ALBIN *crosses to* JEAN-MICHEL, *extending a hand.*)

ALBIN. *(in trembling basso) Bon jour.* It is Indeed it is a pleasure to make your acquaintance.

(JEAN-MICHEL *grabs* ALBIN*'s hand and holds it up for* GEORGES *to see. There is a huge diamond cluster ring on it.*)

JEAN-MICHEL. Papa, look! The crown jewels.

ALBIN. Please. Allow me some comfort.

GEORGES. *(retrieving the ring)* Albin the boy is right. Lets not gild the lily.

(FRANCIS *enters from the club. His arm is now in a sling.*)

FRANCIS. Hey, this is nice. What time's mass?

JEAN-MICHEL. I thought you locked that door.

GEORGES. Francis has a key. Did you need something?

FRANCIS. Sorry. A telegram arrived. *(giving it to* ALBIN*)* I thought it might be important.

ALBIN. *(eyeing the sling)* And what happened to you?

GEORGES. Don't tell me; you and Hanna are engaged.

FRANCIS. *(blushing)* No. But we're getting serious.

(FRANCIS *exits as* GEORGES *crosses to* ALBIN *but* ALBIN *puts the telegram behind him.*)

GEORGES. Bad news?

ALBIN. Just a request for an interview.

(ALBIN *takes the note over to a chair to study it in private.*)

(JEAN-MICHEL *throws his hands up.*)

JEAN-MICHEL. This is never going to work. Crazy people coming in and out. Mother's not here yet.

GEORGES. You must get hold of yourself.

JEAN-MICHEL. It's going to be a disaster.

GEORGES. Not if you keep your wits about you.

JEAN-MICHEL. Papa, I love Anne and I'm going to lose her.

GEORGES. I'll let you in on a little secret, my son. If she loves you, you won't lose her. No matter what happens here.

JEAN-MICHEL. I should have known better. I ask for one lousy favour from him and look. I should have known better. My whole life I've had to put up with his nonsense. When I think of what I've been through because of him. The ribbings I took at school. The beatings I got defending him. The gawking stares every time we left the house because he'd always insist we stroll arm in arm. I'd need a shirt for school, and he'd buy me a blouse.

GEORGES. What about what he's given up for you? The vacations and holidays. The hours helping with your homework. The nights sitting up in your sick room. Have you ever wanted for anything? Private schools. Cars, cash, clothes, anything??? Have you ever asked for anything that you were denied?

JEAN-MICHEL. Yes! How about a little respect for what I want? How about a little understanding?

GEORGES. A little respect? A little understanding?

*[MUSIC NO. 14: **LOOK OVER THERE**]*

HOW OFTEN IS SOMEONE CONCERNED
WITH THE TINIEST THREAD OF YOUR LIFE?
CONCERNED WITH WHATEVER YOU FEEL
AND WHATEVER YOU TOUCH
LOOK OVER THERE
LOOK OVER THERE
SOMEBODY CARES THAT MUCH!

HOW OFTEN DOES SOMEBODY SENSE
THAT YOU NEED THEM WITHOUT BEING TOLD?
WHEN YOU HAVE A HURT IN YOUR HEART

YOU'RE TOO PROUD TO DISCLOSE
LOOK OVER THERE
LOOK OVER THERE
SOMEBODY ALWAYS KNOWS

WHEN YOUR WORLD SPINS TOO FAST
AND YOUR BUBBLE HAS BURST
SOMEONE PUTS HIMSELF LAST
SO THAT YOU CAN COME FIRST

SO COUNT ALL THE LOVES WHO WILL LOVE YOU
FROM NOW TO THE END OF YOUR LIFE
AND WHEN YOU HAVE ADDED THE LOVES
WHO HAVE LOVED YOU BEFORE
LOOK OVER THERE
LOOK OVER THERE
SOMEBODY LOVES YOU MORE

WHEN YOUR WORLD SPINS TOO FAST
AND YOUR BUBBLE HAS BURST
SOMEONE PUTS HIMSELF LAST
SO THAT YOU CAN COME FIRST

(**JEAN-MICHEL** *makes a move toward* **ALBIN**, *but he cannot deal with the conflict between his feelings for* **ALBIN** *and his love for* **ANNE**. *And so he exits, leaving* **GEORGES** *singing, finally, to his* **ALBIN**.)

GEORGES. *(cont.)*
SO COUNT ALL THE LOVES WHO WILL LOVE YOU
FROM NOW TO THE END OF YOUR LIFE
AND WHEN YOU HAVE ADDED THE LOVES
WHO HAVE LOVED YOU BEFORE
LOOK OVER THERE
LOOK OVER THERE

(**ALBIN** *looks over at* **GEORGES** *and just nods.*)

SOMEBODY LOVES YOU MORE!

ALBIN. Oh, poor Jean-Michel.

GEORGES. Poor Jean-Michel?

ALBIN. *(referring to the telegram)* From Sybil. *(reading)* "Dearest darlings. Stop. The Duke proposed. Stop. Off to Amsterdam for a red light district ceremony. Stop. Sorry, Sybil."

GEORGES. *(taking the paper)* Sorry Sybil should be her name.

ALBIN. She's done it to him again.

GEORGES. We'll tell the Dindons that a relative took ill and that Sybil went a' nursing.

ALBIN. And what do we tell the boy?

GEORGES. The truth, no?

ALBIN. Oh, Georges, he'll be so disappointed. No mother.

(The doorbell rings. JEAN-MICHEL runs on in a panic from the kitchen.)

JEAN-MICHEL. They're here! They're here!

(JACOB runs on and joins the panic.)

GEORGES. Take a breath. You'll burst something.

JEAN-MICHEL. It's them! They're at the door and mother is nowhere in sight.

GEORGES. I was thinking; once you're born is a mother really all that important?

(doorbell rings again)

JEAN-MICHEL. Jacob, answer the door.

ALBIN. I can do that.

JEAN-MICHEL. No! Let Jacob do it.

(doorbell rings again)

(JACOB begins to skip merrily toward the door. JEAN-MICHEL grabs his arm and swings him toward the bench.)

On second thought…DOWN!

(All three sit in a line on the bench.)

(JEAN-MICHEL addresses the troops.)

All right, you three. Listen carefully. For the next twenty-one hours there will be people of a lifestyle far removed from the one you live. I beseech you, for the next twenty-one hours to dispense with everything you take pride in and everything that brings you personal joy. My future depends on it.

ALBIN. I was raised a Christian. Humiliation is my lot. They hold a place for me in paradise.

(They all look heavenward. JEAN-MICHEL *starts for the door.)*

JEAN-MICHEL. All right. Now, Papa. You stand over there. And, Albin, please…back there somewhere.

(The doorbell rings again.)

Everybody ready? On your marks. Get set. Go!

[MUSIC NO. 14C: **PRESTO**]

*(*ALBIN *jumps up, screams and runs into the dressing room. Simultaneously,* GEORGES *and* JACOB *jump up and bump into each other.)*

GEORGES. Albin!

*(*JACOB *throws open the door in British Butler manner.)*

(The DINDONS *enter one by one.)*

JACOB. His Excellency The Deputy Dindon.

[MUSIC NO. 14D: **DINDON'S MARCH**]

*(*DINDON *enters confused.)*

Madame Dindon.

(She enters unsure.)

And the Mademoiselle in question.

*(*ANNE *enters charmingly)*

GEORGES. *(approaching* ANNE*)* Charming child. Welcome to our home.

ANNE. Thank you.

DINDON. *(calling her to his side)* Anne!

JEAN-MICHEL. May I present my father.

GEORGES. A pleasure.

DINDON. A pleasure.

MARIE. A pleasure.

ANNE. My pleasure.

GEORGES. Jacob! Fetch the luggage.

(**JACOB** *barks twice and exits.*)

DINDON. Your home makes quite an impression. Yes, that's the word. Impressive. One hardly expects to find this almost monk-like atmosphere in a district notorious for its pleasure palaces.

GEORGES. Yes. It does take some getting used to.

(**JACOB** *throws open the door tossing suitcases into the room.*)

JACOB. Oops!

(*He closes the door, picks up all the cases and exits.*)

MARIE. Is that a nightclub I saw downstairs?

DINDON. Marie, please. (*to* **GEORGES**) Is that a nightclub I saw downstairs?

GEORGES. Oh, I really wouldn't know. It does appear so.

DINDON. And what sort of club would it be?

GEORGES. Oh, I really wouldn't know. We don't associate with that sort of people.

DINDON. And what sort of people would they be?

GEORGES. Oh, I really wouldn't know. They don't go out in the daytime and I was brought up in the dark.

DINDON. I see.

GEORGES. You do?

DINDON. Well, let them frolic while they may. After my election I'll sweep them clean.

GEORGES. And I'll be right behind you with a broomstick.

MARIE. Oh! That crucifix is beautiful. Is it an antique?

GEORGES. It's my father. I mean, it's our father. I mean, my father found it. On an archaeological dig. In a pyramid.

JEAN-MICHEL. Would anyone care for champagne?

DINDON. No, thank you. I leave champagne to those who wish to impress. Myself, I stick to a working man's wine. I am, after all my success, still just an old working man.

GEORGES. Bravo. And is Madame just an old working woman? And I, after all, am just an old Foreign Legionnaire.

[MUSIC NO. 15: COCKTAIL COUNTERPOINT]

JEAN-MICHEL. No, Papa, you were with the French Foreign Service!

GEORGES. Sir!

    I JOINED THE FOREIGN LEGION
    WITH A SABRE IN MY HAND
    AND CRAWLED ACROSS THE DESERT
    WITH MY BELLY IN THE SAND
    WITH MEN WHO LOVED THEIR CAMELS
    AND THEIR BRANDY AND I SWEAR,
    NOBODY DISHED, NOBODY SWISHED
    WHEN I WAS A FOREIGN LEGIONNAIRE.

    (JACOB enters with a tray and plates. JEAN-MICHEL picks up dishes...)

JEAN-MICHEL. Would anyone like an *hors d'oeuvre?*

ANNE. *(passing plates to her mum and dad)* Here. Let me help. Mama, papa.

MARIE. Oh, what adorable dishes. Are these youngsters playing together?

    (JEAN-MICHEL looks at a dish and then charges after JACOB who flees for the kitchen.)

DINDON. They look like Greeks.

GEORGES. *(taking the dish from DINDON)* I assure you there are no Greeks on my plates...unless they weren't washed well.

MARIE. They appear to be young boys, in any case.

GEORGES. I'm certain there are girls too. This is a mixed service.

MARIE.

OH, WHAT LOVELY DISHES THEY'RE SO DELICATE
AND FRAIL
MINE HAVE NAKED PEOPLE I BELIEVE THEY'RE ONLY MALE
OOPS, I THINK THEY'RE PLAYING SOME EXOTIC LITTLE
    GAME

JEAN-MICHEL. *(catching the plate)*

OOPS, I THINK THAT LEAPFROG IS ITS NAME
My mother, the wife of my father, begs your forgiveness. She had to be at the bedside of her sick godmother. She shouldn't be delayed much longer.

GEORGES. How did you know that?

JEAN-MICHEL. She phoned. A little while ago. Anyway, she's very sorry.

(DINDON takes MARIE aside.)

DINDON.

THIS IS EVEN WORSE THAN I FEARED
THE SON IS STRANGE, THE FATHER IS WEIRD
TO MEET THE WIFE, I'M ACTUALLY AFRAID
I PREFER THAT ANNE REMAIN AN OLD MAID

(GEORGES breaks between MARIE and DINDON.)

GEORGES. You know, my wife and I are a devoted couple. Now my son knows how much I love him and to what extremes, but my wife...I love her like an animal.

(MARIE sits breathlessly.)

JEAN-MICHEL. Nibbles. Anyone?

JACOB.

IT'S APPALLING TO CONFESS
OUR NEW IN-LAWS ARE A MESS
SHE'S A PRUDE
HE'S A PRIG
SHE'S A PILL
HE'S A PIG
SO ZIS...
ZIS...
ZIS FOR YOU PAPA!

(all sing together:)

GEORGES.

> I JOINED THE FOREIGN LEGION
> WITH A SABRE IN MY HAND
> AND CRAWLED ACROSS THE DESERT
> WITH MY BELLY IN THE SAND
> WITH MEN WHO LOVED THEIR CAMELS
> AND THEIR BRANDY AND I SWEAR,
> NOBODY DISHED, NOBODY SWISHED
> WHEN I WAS A FOREIGN LEGIONNAIRE.

MARIE.

> OH, WHAT LOVELY DISHES THEY'RE SO DELICATE
> AND FRAIL
> MINE HAVE NAKED PEOPLE I BELIEVE THEY'RE ONLY MALE
> OOPS, I THINK THEY'RE PLAYING SOME EXOTIC LITTLE
>   GAME
> OOPS, I THINK THAT LEAPFROG IS ITS NAME

DINDON.

> THIS IS EVEN WORSE THAN I FEARED
> THE SON IS STRANGE, THE FATHER IS WEIRD
> TO MEET THE WIFE, I'M ACTUALLY AFRAID
> I PREFER THAT ANNE REMAIN AN OLD MAID

JACOB.

> IT'S APPALLING TO CONFESS
> OUR NEW IN-LAWS ARE A MESS
> SHE'S A PRUDE
> HE'S A PRIG
> SHE'S A PILL
> HE'S A PIG
> SO ZIS...
> ZIS...
> ZIS FOR YOU PAPA!
> *(double time!!)*

GEORGES.

> I JOINED THE FOREIGN LEGION
> WITH A SABRE IN MY HAND
> AND CRAWLED ACROSS THE DESERT

WITH MY BELLY IN THE SAND
WITH MEN WHO LOVED THEIR CAMELS
AND THEIR BRANDY AND I SWEAR,
NOBODY DISHED, NOBODY SWISHED
WHEN I WAS A FOREIGN LEGIONNAIRE.

MARIE.

OH, WHAT LOVELY DISHES THEY'RE SO DELICATE
AND FRAIL
MINE HAVE NAKED PEOPLE I BELIEVE THEY'RE ONLY MALE
OOPS, I THINK THEY'RE PLAYING SOME EXOTIC LITTLE
GAME
OOPS, I THINK THAT LEAPFROG IS ITS NAME

DINDON.

THIS IS EVEN WORSE THAN I FEARED
THE SON IS STRANGE, THE FATHER IS WEIRD
TO MEET THE WIFE, I'M ACTUALLY AFRAID
I PREFER THAT ANNE REMAIN AN OLD MAID

JACOB.

IT'S APPALLING TO CONFESS
OUR NEW IN-LAWS ARE A MESS
SHE'S A PRUDE
HE'S A PRIG
SHE'S A PILL
HE'S A PIG
SO ZIS...
ZIS...
ZIS FOR YOU PAPA!

(**ALBIN** *arrives on the musical button. He is dressed as a very proper mother.*)

ALBIN. Here's mother!

(**ALBIN** *approaches his* **GUESTS**.)

I do beg your forgiveness, but my great-uncle was dying and I just had to wait.

DINDON. No apology necessary. But we were led to believe it was your godmother.

ALBIN. And so it was. It was my great-uncle who also served as my godmother since my godmother passed away. God knows what I'll do for a godmother now!

(He laughs.)

MARIE. Let alone a great-uncle! *(joins in laughing)*

*(***JACOB*** exits laughing.)*

JEAN-MICHEL. May I present my mother.

DINDON. Madame.

ALBIN. Dear Sir. *(to* **MARIE***)* Madame. *(sees* **ANNE***)* And the little mademoiselle. Come here. Come here. May I kiss you?

ANNE. Please.

ALBIN. I could be your *Maman.*

JEAN-MICHEL. *(with the tray)* Something to put in your mouth, *Maman?*

ALBIN. Did you wash your hands before serving?

JEAN-MICHEL. *Maman...*

ALBIN. About to be wed, yet still my baby. *(to* **GEORGES***)* Are you not well, darling? You're looking a little ashen.

DINDON. Your husband seemed upset by your absence.

ALBIN. Were you worried, *mon chou?*

GEORGES. I still am.

ALBIN. *(to* **MARIE***)* Oh, what a lovely dress. I just adore comfortable clothing. Believe it or not, before you arrived I was lounging in one of my husband's suits.

GEORGES. More food?

ALBIN. But Georges just hates me in his pants!

GEORGES. I do not hate you in my pants!

JEAN-MICHEL. I think we've had enough *hors d'oeuvres.*

GEORGES. I'll ring for dinner.

JEAN-MICHEL. *(to the heavens)* Please, dear Lord.

*(***GEORGES*** crosses and rings a dinner bell and the kitchen door flies open releasing a cloud of black smoke. ***JACOB*** enters with a tray of blackened chicken. ***ALBIN***

pushes him off stage and turns to the guests.)

ALBIN. We'll be dining out. I hope you don't mind if I take the liberty of choosing a restaurant myself.

DINDON. I don't much care for restaurant food.

ALBIN. Oh, I'm certain the Deputy Dindon will find something to amuse his palate at *Chez Jacqueline.*

MARIE. *Chez Jacqueline!* Did you hear, Edouard?

DINDON. Quiet, Marie.

ALBIN. You've been there, Madame?

MARIE. No. I've been trying to get my husband to take me there for years. *Chez Jacqueline.*

ALBIN. I'm so pleased you're pleased.

DINDON. I understand they're booked months in advance. Just how will you get a reservation?

ALBIN. Never underestimate the ingenuity of a mother. First locate your instrument.

(**JACOB** *enters with a phone on a tray.* **ALBIN** *removes his earring, and lifts the receiver.)*

Next you lift the receiver. Dial the number.

(**JACOB** *dials.)*

And then speak sweetly: Jacqueline? ...*Oui.* I need you. We'll be six.

*[MUSIC NO. 15A: **TO JACQUELINE**]*

SCENE 3

(Chez Jacqueline)

(Music – and a magical transformation. As the apartment and the people in it disappear, the subdued elegance of the restaurant called Chez Jacqueline replaces it.)

(JACQUELINE *enters.*)

JACQUELINE. Welcome to Chez Jacqueline!

ALBIN. How good of you to find room for my little party.

JACQUELINE. For an old friend, anytime. And thank you for accommodating my friends last night. You do know how to put on a show. No one's heard from them since.

GEORGES. *(cutting this off)* Shall we take our seats?

JACQUELINE. Ah, Sir Georges. So dashing. So *distingue!*

GEORGES. Not at all!

JACQUELINE. Come, let me show you to your table.

(She leads them to a banquette.)

DINDON. *(whispers to* MARIE*)* This place is a gold mine. Remind me to have it audited.

JACQUELINE. Voila! I'll send your waiter to you at once. *(to* ALBIN*)* And perhaps, after you've settled in, I can beg a little favour. Yes?

ALBIN. No!

JACQUELINE. *(walking away)* We'll see.

ALBIN. Happy, children?

JEAN-MICHEL. *Oui, Maman.*

DINDON. I have to confess that when Anne announced her intention to be married we were taken by surprise.

GEORGES. As were we.

ALBIN. *(settling in distractedly)* You should have seen the look on Georges' face when Jean-Michel told us he was marrying a woman. I mean, a white woman.

GEORGES. *(trying to cover)* They are, you will admit, quite pale, these young…virgins.

DINDON. I should hope so.

ALBIN. Well, I can account for our son.

DINDON. I don't know if our daughter's told you, but Anne stands to inherit a hefty dowry on her wedding day. Of course, if we approve her choice of husband.

(JACQUELINE takes the stage and calls to all in attendance.)

JACQUELINE. Attention. Attention. *Messieurs-dames.* As those of you who frequent our little establishment know, we count many celebrities and heads of state among our treasured clientele. And I would never think of disturbing their privacy by introducing them. BUT tonight, I cannot resist because among you sits one of my favourite people on this earth. Someone who has made their own unique place in the world and from there spreads happiness to us all.

MARIE. Edouard, she's going to introduce you.

DINDON. Please Marie. I have ears.

JACQUELINE. Messieurs-dames, lift your glass with me to toast a singular individual…

(DINDON begins to rise…)

The one and only Zaza!

(JACQUELINE turns to ALBIN.)

(DINDON sits.)

JEAN-MICHEL. Goodbye wedding.

DINDON. Zaza! You? An actress?

ALBIN. Oh, it's nothing I took seriously. Just a pastime, a hobby.

GEORGES. She tried her hand at bowling, but singing seemed to suit her better.

JACQUELINE. After an introduction like that I'm certain we can persuade Zaza to favour us with a little song.

ALBIN. Thank you, Jacqueline, but no. I've given all that up. I'm just a mother now.

JACQUELINE. Another miracle at Lourdes?

MARIE. Well, I'd love to hear you sing if anyone wants my vote.

DINDON. No one does. Sit down.

JACQUELINE. Oh, please, Zaza. Just one little *chanson.* I won't take no for an answer. I will stand here and badger you all night.

JEAN-MICHEL. Perhaps you'd better, Mother.

ALBIN. If you insist, *cherie.*

JACQUELINE. Oh, but I do. G?

ALBIN. G flat. I've had a child.

JACQUELINE. *(backing away) Merci, mille fois.*

ALBIN. I would like to dedicate this song to someone very special: Dear Anne, welcome, dear child, to our family. *(to the band)* Maestro, *je suis dispose.*

*[MUSIC NO. 16: **BEST OF TIMES**]*

(He turns with the music and sings.)

THIS IS A LITTLE SONG
NOSTALGIC AND UNIQUE
I LEARN TO SING THIS SONG BEFORE I COULD SPEAK-EH
I LEARNED TO SING THIS SONG UPON MY MOTHER'S KNEE
AND SHE LEARNED TO SING THIS SONG
UPON HER MOTHER'S KNEE
AND HER MOTHER LEARNED THIS SONG
UPON HER MOTHER'S KNEE

(GEORGES *coughs to interrupt a carried away* **ALBIN.** *)*

AND IF YOUR MOTHER SANG THIS LITTLE SONG TO YOU
Then sing along with me…

(front:)

THE BEST OF TIMES IS NOW
WHAT'S LEFT OF SUMMER BUT A FADED ROSE?
THE BEST OF TIMES IS NOW

AS FOR TOMORROW, WELL, WHO KNOWS,
WHO KNOWS,
WHO KNOWS?

SO HOLD THIS MOMENT FAST
AND LIVE AND LOVE AS HARD AS YOU KNOW HOW
AND MAKE THIS MOMENT LAST
BECAUSE THE BEST OF TIMES IS NOW
IS NOW
IS NOW!

NOW!
NOT SOME FORGOTTEN YESTERDAY
NOW!
TOMORROW IS TOO FAR AWAY

SO HOLD THIS MOMENT FAST
AND LIVE AND LOVE AS HARD AS YOU KNOW HOW
AND MAKE THIS MOMENT LAST
BECAUSE THE BEST OF TIMES IS NOW
IS NOW
IS NOW!

JACQUELINE.
THE BEST OF TIMES IS NOW
WHAT'S LEFT OF SUMMER BUT A FADED ROSE?

ALBIN & JACQUELINE.
THE BEST OF TIMES IS NOW
AS FOR TOMORROW, WELL

JACQUELINE.
WHO KNOWS?

ALBIN.
WHO KNOWS?

ALBIN & JACQUELINE.
WHO KNOWS?

(with more gusto)

SO HOLD THIS MOMENT FAST
AND LIVE AND LOVE AS HARD AS YOU KNOW HOW
AND MAKE THIS MOMENT LAST
BECAUSE THE BEST OF TIMES

JACQUELINE.

IS NOW

ALBIN.

IS NOW

ALBIN & JACQUELINE.

IS NOW!

COLETTE.

IS NOW!

TABARRO.

IS NOW!

*(The song is infectious, and drawn in by **ALBIN** and **JACQUELINE**, the **OTHERS** sing, too.)*

ALBIN & JACQUELINE.

NOW...!

WAITER.

...NOW!

ALBIN, JACQUELINE & CHORUS.

NOT SOME FORGOTTEN YESTERDAY...

ETIENNE.

...YESTERDAY

ALBIN, JACQUELINE & CHORUS.

NOW...!

ANNE.

...NOW!

ALBIN, JACQUELINE & CHORUS.

TOMORROW IS TOO FAR AWAY

*(**MARIE** rises and sings.)*

MARIE.

SO HOLD THIS MOMENT FAST
AND LIVE AND LOVE AS HARD AS YOU KNOW HOW

*(**DINDON** glares at **MARIE** and she and **ANNE** sit back down as **ALBIN** pinches back the followspot.)*

ALL.

AND MAKE THIS MOMENT LAST
BECAUSE THE BEST OF TIMES IS NOW

IS NOW
IS NOW!

(GEORGES rises and embraces ALBIN, and then helps MARIE up. MARIE dances with GEORGES.)

THE BEST OF TIMES IS NOW
WHAT'S LEFT OF SUMMER BUT A FADED ROSE?
THE BEST OF TIMES IS NOW
AS FOR TOMORROW, WELL, WHO KNOWS,
WHO KNOWS,
WHO KNOWS?

(JEAN-MICHEL and ANNE are up.)

SO HOLD THIS MOMENT FAST
AND LIVE AND LOVE AS HARD AS YOU KNOW HOW
AND MAKE THIS MOMENT LAST
BECAUSE THE BEST OF TIMES IS NOW
IS NOW
IS NOW!

(DINDON rises, getting into the spirit, and dances with JACQUELINE.)

NOW!
NOT SOME FORGOTTEN YESTERDAY
NOW!
TOMORROW IS TOO FAR AWAY.

(Polka starts and DINDON starts to dance with ALBIN.)

SO HOLD THIS MOMENT FAST
AND LIVE AND LOVE AS HARD AS YOU KNOW HOW
AND MAKE THIS MOMENT LAST

BECAUSE THE BEST OF TIMES IS NOW
IS NOW
IS NOW!

(ALL clapping in rhythm.)

SO HOLD THIS MOMENT FAST
AND LIVE AND LOVE AS HARD AS YOU KNOW HOW
AND MAKE THIS MOMENT LAST
BECAUSE THE BEST OF TIMES IS NOW
IS NOW

IS NOW!
IS NOW!

[MUSIC NO. 16A: **BEST OF TIMES PLAYOFFF/**
FURIES CHASE*]*

(It's one of those rare, glorious moments when everyone
is really having the time of his life. And the triumph,
of course, is **MOTHER ALBIN***'s. "Brava, Zaza! Brava!"*
EVERYONE *cries and applauds.)*

(And **ALBIN,** *ever the star, back in her element, curtsies*
and curtsies, and ends, as she always does, with her
habitual gesture: She takes off her wig. And freezes in
horror.)

ALBIN. Oh, merde!

(DINDON *also freezes in horror. Then he starts to run*
Stage Left. A **BIRD** *from La Cage Aux Folles enters and*
stops him.)

DINDON. La Cage Aux Folles!

(He runs stage right, stage left, upstage, downstage and
gets stopped by a bird at every turn)

ALL those shameful young men! Gendarme!
Gendarme! Help me!! Help me!! Cults, cats, punks,
perverts!

(The lights go berserk: a fantastic nightmare. The
restaurant disappears and the walls of the apartment
come in closing around the **DINDONS** *and the others.)*

SCENE 4

(The Apartment)

(**JEAN-MICHEL, GEORGES,** *and the* **DINDONS** *have arrived breathless.* **ALBIN** *sits quietly poised.)*

DINDON. To think–to think that a daughter of mine would get herself involved with filth like this.

MARIE. Edouard!

DINDON. It's all your fault, Marie.

MARIE. My fault?

GEORGES. I say lets call it a night, go to bed, and start out fresh in the morning.

DINDON. Homosexual!

ALBIN. Perhaps we should sit out this round.

MARIE. March on, Edouard. Lead us out of this house of sin. We are right behind you.

ANNE. Sorry, Mother, but we are not right behind you. I'm staying here with Jean-Michel and we're getting married.

DINDON. Dare to defy me and I will cut you off without a sou!

ANNE. Cut me off. Do you think I brought you here just to get a dowry?

DINDON. You mean you knew about these people?

ANNE. No. But now that I do, it doesn't matter. I like them.

DINDON. HOMOSEXUALS!

ANNE. Father, don't bellow. They know what they are.

DINDON. Young lady, you march yourself straight out that door.

ANNE. No. I love you Father. *(to* **MARIE***)* You too, mother. You are my family. But I love Jean-Michel. So we are going to marry and start our own family.

DINDON. And what sort of family do you think this son of a pervert could make, being brought up as he was by two transvestite homosexuals?

ALBIN. One transvestite.

GEORGES. One plain homosexual.

(**JEAN-MICHEL** *finally steps forward.*)

JEAN-MICHEL. Deputy Dindon, I must apologise for everything that happened here tonight. I made a terrible mistake but I'm going to spend the rest of my life trying to make up for it. And I hope to one day receive forgiveness for being stupid and thoughtless.

DINDON. While I appreciate the sentiments, I do not accept your apology.

JEAN-MICHEL. That's quite all right as it wasn't to you I was apologising. It was to my parents.

DINDON. Your parents? What parents? Oh, one of them could have possibly fathered you, but you can't tell me that the other one is your mother.

JEAN-MICHEL. That's precisely who he is.

*[MUSIC NO. 16B: **LOOK OVER THERE–REPRISE**]*

DINDON. I see no mother here.

JEAN-MICHEL. *(to* **ALBIN***)* I do.

HOW OFTEN IS SOMEONE CONCERNED
WITH THE TINIEST THREAD OF YOUR LIFE?
CONCERNED WITH WHATEVER YOU FEEL
AND WHATEVER YOU TOUCH?
LOOK OVER THERE
LOOK OVER THERE
SOMEBODY CARES THAT MUCH

SO COUNT ALL THE LOVES WHO WILL LOVE ME
FROM NOW TO THE END OF MY LIFE
AND WHEN YOU HAVE ADDED THE LOVES
WHO HAVE LOVED ME BEFORE
LOOK OVER THERE

JEAN-MICHEL & GEORGES.

LOOK OVER THERE.
SOMEBODY LOVES ME/YOU MORE!

(ALBIN joins with GEORGES and JEAN-MICHEL for a family hug.)

DINDON. Marie, they are all insane. Let's get out of here before they turn on us.

(At that JACOB enters with their luggage.)

JACOB. Here's a fun idea; you get the bags and I'll get the door. *Oui?*

(And JACOB tosses the luggage to the floor.)

DINDON. Marie, bags!

(JACOB pulls the door open to reveal JACQUELINE.)

JACQUELINE. Ah, there you are, Deputy Dindon. You all came and went so quickly I didn't even realise who you were. Naughty little Zaza. You should have told me who he was.

ALBIN. Somehow I knew you'd figure it out.

JACQUELINE. And somehow I did! And once I realised who you were I said to myself, "Jacqueline," I said, "Here comes, and there goes, the famous Deputy Dindon and you didn't even get your picture taken with him." And that made Jacqueline so sad. And then I thought, "Jacqueline, seeing as how he left in such a hurry, without even paying his bill, I'm certain that he wouldn't mind my inviting a few of the newspapers and television stations to an impromptu photo session with his old friend Jacqueline." So here we are. The press awaits outside.

DINDON. Newspapers?

JACQUELINE. Uh-huh.

DINDON. Television stations?

JACQUELINE. Mm-hm!

DINDON. I'll be ruined.

JACQUELINE. But of course.

ALBIN. Oh, Jacqueline, you are such a star ffff...ollower.

JACQUELINE. Now, Zaza, there is more to running a successful restaurant than good food. I always say, "A little publicity can do more good than a delicious sauce."

GEORGES. And having your picture taken with the most famous anti-homosexual on the Riviera alongside the most infamous homosexual on the Riviera...

JACQUELINE. Now that's a delicious sauce.

GEORGES & ALBIN. Brava, Jacqueline.

(ALBIN *approaches* DINDON.)

ALBIN. Deputy Ding Dong...

DINDON. The name is Dindon.

ALBIN. Be nice.

GEORGES. I believe we can help you out of this awkward situation.

DINDON. You can? How?

GEORGES. But first, Albin and I have been discussing the matter and we've decided to give our blessings to the union of our two children.

ALBIN. We think you should do the same. Don't you?

DINDON. Never! Do you hear? Never!

(DINDON *runs to the door and* JACOB *throws it open. Flashbulbs explode in his face.* JACOB *slams it shut.*)

They have my blessing.

GEORGES. And about the dowry...?

DINDON. The dowry is hers. What more do you want?

ALBIN. On those occasions when you're invited to family gatherings; Christmas, birthdays, anniversaries, could you do us a small favour?

DINDON. We'll come.

ALBIN. Don't!

DINDON. Very well. It's a deal.

ALBIN. *(to the kids)* Congratulations.

JEAN-MICHEL. *(kissing* ALBIN*)* Thank you, *Maman.*

ANNE. *(kissing* **ALBIN**) Thank you, *Maman.*

ALBIN. *Maman. (crosses to* **MARIE***) Maman*

JACQUELINE. And how about me?

GEORGES. Jacqueline?

ALBIN. Jacqueline.

JACQUELINE. Jacqueline! Yes, you all forgot about Jacqueline.

ALBIN. And we wouldn't want to do that after all she's done for us, would we?

GEORGES. Jacob? Escort Jacqueline out to the photographers and say we'll join them in a moment. Jacqueline, I trust you'll keep the gentlemen entertained while we freshen up.

JACQUELINE. You can count on me. *(to* **DINDON***) En garde!*

(**JACOB** *opens the door for* **JACQUELINE***'s grand exit into the flashbulbs, and shuts it after her.*)

GEORGES. Did you lock it?

JACOB. *Maman* didn't raise no fool.

(**EVERYONE,** *except* **DINDON,** *laughs.*)

DINDON. Well, I'm glad to see you are all enjoying yourselves. Meanwhile I'm right back to where I started: Blackmail to the left of me, betrayal to the right, ruination in front of me and God knows what in the rear. Help me.

GEORGES. I think I know one way out.

DINDON. Tell me. Take me. I'll do anything.

(**ALBIN** *leads* **DINDON,** **JEAN-MICHEL** *leads* **ANNE,** **JACOB** *leads* **MARIE** *as they exit.*)

SCENE 5

*[MUSIC NO. 16C: **AU REVOIR**]*

(**GEORGES** *steps forward as the stage becomes La Cage in preparation for the finale.*)

GEORGES. Lights

Curtain

And it's just *vous et moi*

IT'S RATHER GAUDY,

BUT IT'S ALSO RATHER GRAND

AND WHILE THE WAITER PADS YOUR CHEQUE HE'LL KISS YOUR HAND

THE CLEVER GIGOLOS ROMANCE THE WEALTHY MATRONS

AT LA CAGE AUX FOLLES

Ah bon soir Harry, and Duchess is that you? I didn't recognise you behind the moustache. It brings out your eyes. And Marcel, you've had your hair straightened. What? You did it yourself? Marvellous the things one learns in prison!

YOU GO ALONE TO HAVE THE EVENING OF YOUR LIFE

YOU MEET YOUR MISTRESS

AND YOUR BOYFRIEND AND YOUR WIFE

IT'S A BONANZA IT'S A MAD EXTRAVAGANZA

AT LA CAGE AUX FOLLES....

And so, my friends, once again the inevitable is upon us. It is time to bring our entertainment to a close. Time for all the pieces that have flown apart to come back together again. And, if we have done our jobs correctly, you will leave with more than a folded program and a torn ticket stub.

Messieurs-dames! La Cage Aux Folles proudly presents our Finale, featuring a cornucopia of tasty morsels from our home grown garden of delights. And, as an extra added one time only surprise, some of the newest, most promising and oddest talent ever to appear in cabaret.

Ladies and Gentlemen, hold on to your seats. Maestro, if you please!

*[MUSIC NO. 17: **FINALE**]*

(music plays)

CAGELLES.

AHHHHHHHHH *(etc.)*

(The show curtain rises on **CAGELLES** *and* **GEORGES**.*)*

GEORGES.

LIFE IS A CELEBRATION
WITH YOU ON MY ARM
WALKING'S A NEW SENSATION
WITH YOU ON MY ARM
EACH TIME I FACE A MORNING
THAT'S BORING AND BLAND
WITH YOU IT LOOKS GOOD
WITH YOU IT LOOKS GREAT
WITH YOU IT LOOKS GRAND
SOMEHOW YOU'VE PUT A PERMANENT STAR IN MY EYE
EVEN THE DEAD OF WINTER CAN FEEL LIKE JULY
I FOUND A COMBINATION THAT WORKS LIKE A CHARM
IT'S SUDDENLY, OOH!
IT'S SUDDENLY, LA!
WHENEVER IT'S YOU
IT'S YOU
IT'S YOU
IT'S YOU...

And now, introducing the stars of tomorrow!

Presenting the last of the vestal virgins. Innocent, virtuous and chaste...by every boy in town.

Ann-Genue!

*(**ANNE** appears.)*

And now, the temptress of the tropics. She's made of sugar and spice and ev-e-ry vice...Jacobina!

*(**JACOB** appears at last in the show only to fall flat on his beaded face. He's crestfallen.)*

GEORGES. *(cont.)* Perhaps we'll try again tomorrow.

(**JACOB** *looks up at* **GEORGES** *with glee and blows him a kiss*)

And now welcome a siren for every season. A surprise in every sense, Ave Maria! ·

(**MME. DINDON** *enters and she's a knockout in a most revealing outfit*)

And lastly, what family doesn't have one? The woman no man can ever forget! Hard as he tries. One look in her eyes and men flee gratefully home to their wives! I give you, Winhilda!

(**DINDON** *appears as the ugliest woman ever.*)

(*Rumba music blares forth and the* **DINDONS** *and* **JACOB** *are swept up by the company and dance along.*)

ALL.

LA LA LA
LA LA LA LA LA LA LA LA
LA LA LA
LA LA LA LA LA LA LA LA

LA LA LA LA LA LA LA LA
LA LA LA LA LA LA LA LA LA LA LA

LA LA LA
LA LA LA LA LA LA LA
LA LA LA
LA LA LA LA LA LA LA

LA LA LA LA LA LA LA LA
LA LA LA LA LA LA LA LA LA LA LA

YOU GO ALONE TO HAVE THE EVENING OF YOUR LIFE
YOU MEET YOUR MISTRESS AND YOUR BOYFRIEND AND
    YOUR WIFE
THE JOY'S CONTAGIOUS

(*During this* **JACQUELINE**, *followed by bulb flashing* **PHOTOGRAPHERS**, *chase through the audience toward the stage.*)

YOU CAN BRING YOUR WHOLE OUTRAGEOUS ENTOURAGE
(OUTRAGEOUS ENTOURAGE)
(OUTRAGEOUS ENTOURAGE)
ENTOURAGE!

(**GEORGES** *points* **JACQUELINE** *off in the wrong direction as* **LES CAGELLES** *sweep the* **DINDONS** *away to safety.*)

IT'S HOT AND HECTIC
EFFERVESCENT AND ECLECTIC
AT LA CAGE AUX FOLLES!

(*But* **JEAN-MICHEL** *returns to the stage and kisses* **GEORGES** *on both cheeks with deep gratitude. He turns and rejoins* **ANNE**, *and they escape hand in hand.*)

(**GEORGES** *is alone on the stage. Satisfied, but saddened by the loss of his son.*)

(*The music shifts to* **SONG ON THE SAND**. **ALBIN** *appears singing softly…*)

ALBIN.
THOUGH THE TIME TUMBLES BY
THERE IS ONE THING THAT I AM FOREVER
CERTAIN OF
I HEAR LA DA DA DA DA DA DA…

GEORGES.
LA DA DA DA DA DA DA
DA DA DA DA DA DA DA

GEORGES & ALBIN.
AND I'M YOUNG AND IN LOVE!

(**GEORGES** *joins* **ALBIN** *and they kiss*)

(*The curtain falls.*)

[MUSIC NO. 18: **BOWS**]

THE BEST OF TIMES IS NOW
WHAT'S LEFT OF SUMMER BUT A FADED ROSE?
THE BEST OF TIMES IS NOW
AS FOR TOMORROW, WELL, WHO KNOWS,

WHO KNOWS,
WHO KNOWS?

SO HOLD THIS MOMENT FAST
AND LIVE AND LOVE AS HARD AS YOU KNOW HOW
AND MAKE THIS MOMENT LAST
BECAUSE THE BEST OF TIMES IS NOW
IS NOW
IS NOW!

SO HOLD THIS MOMENT FAST
AND LIVE AND LOVE AS HARD AS YOU KNOW HOW
AND MAKE THIS MOMENT LAST
BECAUSE THE BEST OF TIMES IS NOW
IS NOW
IS NOW!

(curtain down)

JERRY HERMAN (Composer and Lyricist). *Hello, Dolly!*, *Mame*, and *La Cage Aux Folles* are home to some of the most popular, most-often performed and most successful musical hero(in)es of all time, and have given Jerry Herman the distinction of being the only composer-lyricist in history to have had three musicals that ran more than 1,500 consecutive performances on Broadway. His first Broadway show was *Milk and Honey* (1961), followed by *Hello, Dolly!* (1964), *Mame* (1966), *Dear World* (1969), *Mack & Mabel* (1974), *The Grand Tour* (1979), *La Cage Aux Folles* (1983), *Jerry's Girls* (1985) and "Mrs. Santa Claus" (1996), a CBS TV special starring Angela Lansbury. *Showtune*, a revue of his life's work, is performing in regional theatres around the country and two of Jerry's classic songs are the emotional highlights of the hit Disney-Pixar film *WALL-E*. His string of awards and honors includes multiple Tony Awards, Grammys, Olivier Awards, Drama Desk Awards, the Johnny Mercer Award, the Richard Rodgers Award, the Oscar Hammerstein Award, the Frederick Lowe Award, the Songwriters Hall of Fame, the Theatre Hall of Fame and most recently The Kennedy Center Honors.

HARVEY FIERSTEIN (Librettist). Harvey Fierstein made his professional acting debut at La Mama ETC in 1971 in Andy Warhol's only play, *Pork*. He followed that with appearances in more than 60 Off-Off-Broadway productions before he began his playwriting career. Early plays like *Flatbush Tosca* and *Cobra Jewels* led to his underground hit, *Torch Song Trilogy*, which transferred Off-Broadway in 1981, and then to Broadway in 1982 where it won the Best Play Tony Award, among others. Fierstein also won Tony, Drama Desk, and Theater World acting awards for his portrayal of the lead. Fierstein won his third Tony for the libretto of the musical *La Cage Aux Folles*, which is the only show in history to have won Best Musical and two Best Revival of a Musical Tony Awards. His other plays include Newsies (Tony nominated for Best Book), *Kinky Boots* (Tony nominated for Best Book), *A Catered Affair* (Drama League winner Outstanding Musical of the Year), *Safe Sex*, *Spookhouse*, *Legs Diamond*, and *Casa Valentina* (Tony nominated for Best Play).

As a Broadway actor, Fierstein's starring role as Edna in the musical *Hairspray* won him a fourth Tony Award. Other highlights include a triumphant year on Broadway as Tevye in *Fiddler on the Roof*, and his 2011 portrayal of Albin in the Broadway revival of *La Cage Aux Folles*. His television work includes "Nurse Jackie," "The Good Wife," "How I Met Your Mother," "Family Guy," and "The Simpsons." Films include *Mrs. Doubtfire*, *Independence Day*, *Death to Smoochy*, *Bullets Over Broadway*, and the Academy Award and Emmy Award winning documentary, *The Times of Harvey Milk*.

Fierstein was inducted into the Theater Hall of Fame in 2008. His children's book, *The Sissy Duckling*, is published by Simon & Schuster and the HBO film version won him the Humanitas Prize. As a social and political commentator, Harvey's opinion pieces and essays have been featured on the TV series "In the Life," and on the Op-Ed pages of the *New York Times* and *Huffington Post* among other publications.